THE THINGS OF NATURE

BOOK ONE

MOLLY JANE

Copyright © 2024 by Molly Jane

All rights reserved. This book or any portion thereof may not be reproduced or used in any manner whatsoever without the express written permission of the publisher except for the use of brief quotations in a book review.

Printed in the United States of America

First Printing, 2024

ISBN: 979-8-89316-974-4 (paperback)
ISBN: 979-8-89316-973-7 (ebook)

Editor: Melanie Demmer

Cover Design By GetCovers

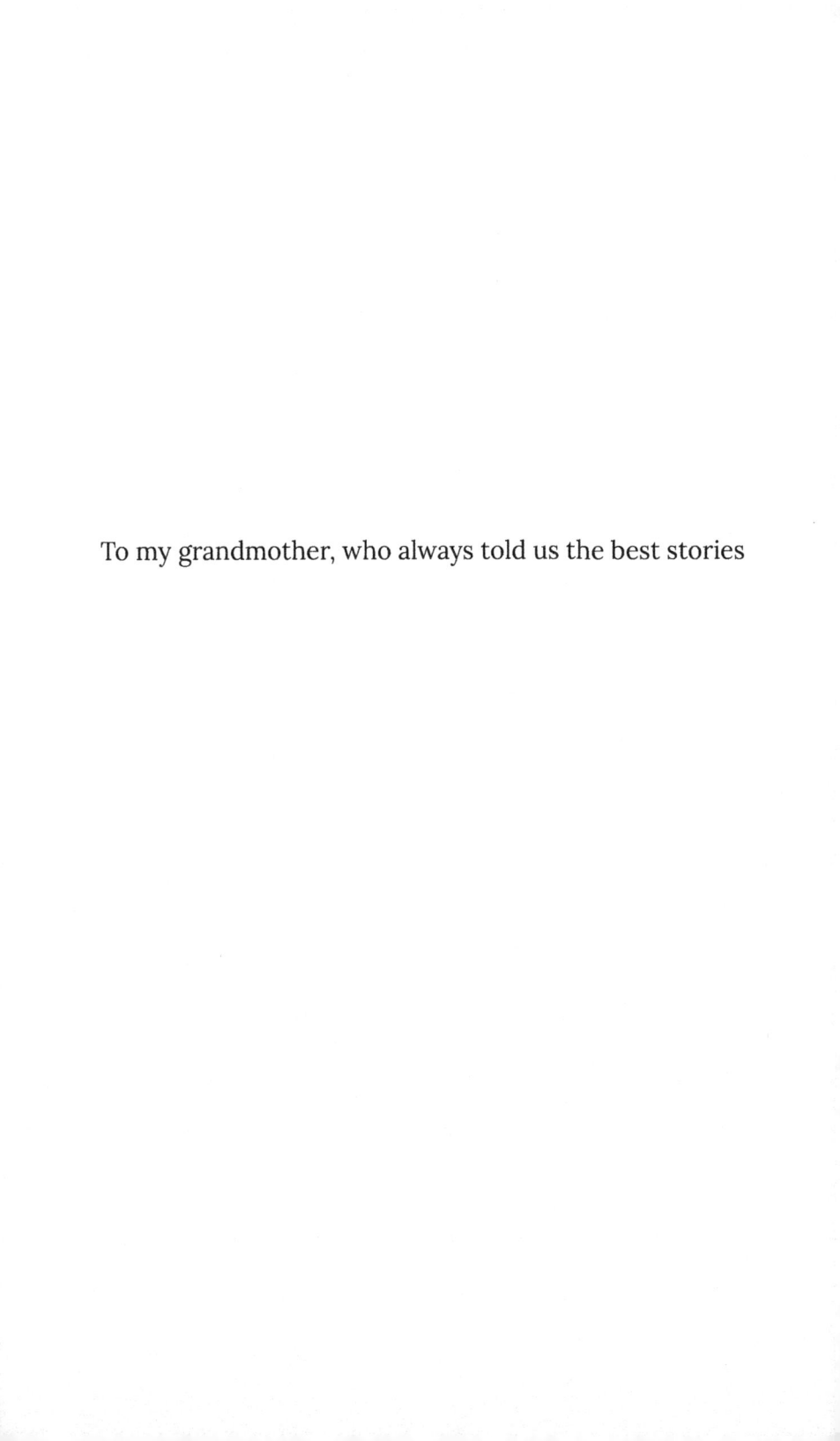

To my grandmother, who always told us the best stories

Want to read a novella for free?
Find out about Reuben and the beginning of his journey.
Simply join my newsletter here to join my mailing list and claim your free copy of this novella!
www.authormollyjane.com

Chapter 1

The newly fallen inch of snow covered the small village, a blanket of quiet that made the night brighter. It wasn't cold. No breeze blew or disturbed the scene. The silence was comfortable, and I would normally have felt calm and at ease at a time like that. But there was no way I could calm my heart or the anticipation that coursed through me.

I continued my slow walk, past the darkened windows and the dwindling smoke from the chimneys. The only sound I could hear was the crunching of the soft snow beneath my boots on the cobblestones, and every now and again, the creak of an old tree branch laden with a new weight.

I exited the village, passing beyond the iron gate. It always stood open, never needing to close. Under the snow, I knew the path turned to dirt. Trees lined the side of the road, and they cast their shadows from the light of the moon.

I wrapped my jacket tighter around me, not from the cold, but to protect what I was holding underneath. The scent of sweet daisies rose from inside my jacket, and the paper crinkled loudly, reminding me of what was at stake.

I was almost there, and my mind rolled and pitched with all the possibilities. So many things could go wrong. But I had made up my mind. I was going to tell her everything.

I turned off the main road and hurried down a small path. It was invisible under the new snow, but I knew the way by heart from the look of the trees and rocks nearby. A soft light emerged ahead, and its soft warmth immediately relaxed me. The small cabin rose before me, its windows alight from the fire within. It was so familiar. It was home.

I released the flowers from underneath my coat as I walked up the two small steps of the porch. Normally, I would have let myself in, but instead, I took in a shaky breath and knocked.

"Calum, I'm home," I called, trying to instill some confidence in my voice, which was rough from misuse. There was no answering call from that sweet voice. Maybe she had fallen asleep.

I opened the door slowly and shut it behind me as I stepped in, stamping off my boots on the mat. The fire was dwindling and not at its climax like I had expected. The rocking chair before it was empty, and the small kitchen was spotless, just like her. Even though we had so little, we put great care into keeping things tidy.

THE THINGS OF NATURE

I placed the flowers gingerly on the wooden counter and passed through the cozy room to head up the stairs. The upstairs has two rooms, unlike the one larger room downstairs. Six years ago, it had been a single room, but then I had found her and everything had changed.

I peeked into her room, expecting to find her small form curled up beneath her wool blanket, her curls peeking out from beneath the covers. The blanket was folded neatly, untouched.

My heart immediately dropped, and I called quickly, "Calum?"

Then with more urgency in my voice when there was no answer, "Calum?"

Something was wrong. Something was terribly, terribly wrong. She should have been there. She never left on her own at night. My palms were beginning to sweat.

A page of stationery lay folded on her small desk, and I snatched it. A note! The words that I read broke me: *Adric, I'm sorry. I hope you'll understand.*

Before the paper fluttered to the ground, I was out the door.

⋄⇌◯⇋⋄

Calum found her favorite spot. Even with the new snow, she could still detect the jutted-out edge of rock about twenty feet up the side of the cliff. She sat with her back against it and shoved her bare fingers into her armpits, trying to warm them after the small climb. Her breath billowed out in front of her and the moon shone bright upon the forest below her, making the trees and shadows lifeless colors of gray and black.

She sighed and closed her eyes. She was there for a reason.

She did not want to be a burden anymore. She was so tired of the guilt, the constant nagging feeling of uselessness. While he hunted for furs to pay for their needs, she sat at home, hidden away from the world. It was for the best that she left. With her gone, there would be no more sparse meals for Adric, no more hungry days. She would never have to feel that guilt again or look into his eyes as he apologized, his eyes full of sadness.

It was for the best.

The shivers came as the warmth from her small hike faded. The spasms raked her body, and she pulled her knees to her chest, trying to hold herself together. Time passed. It felt like a century, but she was getting used to the cold.

She continued to try to convince herself. He would be so much better off without an extra mouth to feed. She simply cared about him too much, and leaving was the only option she could think of to make things better.

The night was setting in deep and dark, and she let her mind wander. She couldn't feel her toes anymore, or the tips of her ears. Hopefully, it wouldn't be too much longer before she lost all feeling.

Then there were arms wrapping around her.

"Calum." His voice was gentle, and for a spark of a moment, she felt relief. He had come for her. But that quickly turned into disappointment. That had not been the plan.

Opening her eyes, she saw his flushed cheeks, his heavy breathing, and his hair falling into his eyes, which searched hers with concern. She closed her own to block them out.

"I don't know what you're doing. I'm taking you home." His voice was firm, frustrated, and he hurried to scoop her up into his arms.

⋅➤⟠◯⟠⟵⋅

I wasn't sure I had made it in time, but she had still been breathing when I arrived. She was even conscious. It was a relief to find she hadn't been out there for too long alone. I was still frustrated and confused; but mostly confused. It made no sense to me at all. I had no idea what was going through her mind.

Before this had happened, I thought everything was fine. We chatted every day. She would tell me about the books she was reading, and I would tell her about gossip from the town. I taught her how to garden and cook and we lived happily and peacefully. I had always helped her out with anything she needed. But the trek up the mountain was going to change everything.

When I found her a few hours before, a soft dust of white had collected on her hair and eyelashes. It hadn't been hard to find her in her favorite spot. Maybe there was some small piece inside of her that wanted me to find her. It was so easy. I just couldn't understand why she would even do it. If she wanted to tell me something, she should have just talked to me. I thought we were closer than that. I thought we told each other everything. We were best friends. It was us against the world.

I sat in the rocker by the fire, staring at her sleeping form, watching her breathe softly, her chest rising and falling. I reached out and touched her fingers. Still cold. I drew back.

She had fallen asleep instantly once I set up the cot. I hadn't moved since. All I had done was pull off her boots and check for frostbite. Her fingers had luckily been fine, tucked under her arms the whole time. But her small nose, ears, and toes were a violent red in the warm room. It made my chest ache.

If only I had come home sooner. If only I hadn't been so occupied with worrying about telling her how I felt, then I might have noticed her acting differently. I thought she was happy there with me. But maybe she felt trapped in the small cabin in the woods. Maybe she had run from me for some reason. That was my worst fear.

I placed my head in my hands, shutting my eyes.

When I found her all those years ago, she had been so small, skinny, dirty. She had been lost in the woods, scared and alone. She had been no more than twelve, perhaps, and I had been about seventeen. At that time, my parents had been dead for several years, and I had inherited the cabin in the woods. I had continued the hunting business, setting traps mostly, sometimes using my bow if I was in a sporting mood. It had been one of those days of setting out traps when I found her. I had startled her, but she hadn't run. Perhaps because I was still not fully grown, barely an adult myself. I immediately invited her to the cabin. I had been lonely, and I knew I could hide her from whatever she was running from. She had followed, eyeing me warily. But she had followed, nonetheless. It took a while for me to earn her trust, but she needed someone. She was hungry and alone.

I assumed that she had run away from something, maybe her previous home. A little girl wouldn't run away from nothing into the unknown wilderness, dressed in barely a rag, her hair a tangled mess and her eyes hard. She had always evaded my questions on the subject, and, therefore, I knew nothing of her past.

I looked up again at her sleeping form and checked the fire to make sure it was still crackling strong. Her curly, golden hair was straggly and damp instead of vibrant; her eyes sunken in. Her cheeks were still too pale and contrasted sharply with the angry red of her nose.

The night passed, and she didn't wake until the next morning when her eyes slowly opened, dreary from sleep. I had picked up a book in the late hours, but quickly put it down upon noticing her move.

Her eyes looked around for a moment as if she were lost, then they focused on the window, probably checking what time of day it was. Then, they came to rest on me. Our eyes remained locked, until she turned away, closing hers again, and I could feel my frustration rising. I wouldn't let her ignore me.

"Calum, why did you leave?" It came out more frustrated than I had wanted to sound, but it got her attention.

"I'm sorry," she whispered softly.

"I just don't understand why you didn't come to me first." I could feel the exasperation welling up inside of me. I needed her to speak to me and help me understand.

"You're lucky I came home early, and I'm glad you were in the first place I checked. Calum, what were you doing? Were you trying to run away?" My tone was full of bewilderment.

"I'm sorry," she said again, as if she were trying to push me away.

A deep sigh rumbled out of me as I tried to release my frustration.

I lightly placed my rough hand on her ice-cold fingers. I spoke gently, feeling sorry that I had raised my voice. "Please, tell me." I wanted to know what was wrong, not to make the argument worse. I was confused, sure, but I needed clarity.

Glancing in my direction, she whispered, "I just . . . I'm a burden to you, Adric. You do so much for me, and I just feel useless. I don't know." She tried to gauge my reaction. I was shocked.

"Why would you think such a thing, Calum? That's not true at all!"

My heart felt like it was sinking into my toes, and I was desperate for her to understand.

"It is!" Her eyes looked imploringly into mine. "It is true! You are always taking care of me, and because of me, there's barely enough to eat. And you can't bring anyone home with me here. I'm in the way." Her agonized eyes turned away from mine toward the window. "I'm in the way of you having a life."

"That's not true, Calum. The thought of you as a burden never crossed my mind." My heart beat so hard in my chest I thought it might exit my body. I couldn't believe she felt this way. We were supposed to be a team. I thought she knew that.

"Are those flowers?" Her question threw me off and I blinked, my mind churning back to earlier in the night, and I quickly realized where she was looking.

"I thought you might like them," I responded, not able to tell her the whole truth. Not then. I thought maybe she felt the same toward me, but perhaps I was wrong. I must have projected some of my emotions onto her.

I thought our relationship had transformed from when we first met. We were more like siblings at the beginning. Maybe she still saw me as an older brother and nothing more. I couldn't believe I had been so wrong. I was in love with her now. I couldn't deny it. I began to feel it around a year before, and ever since then, I have been unable to go back to how I felt earlier.

I finally broke the wary silence. "You should get some more rest. I'm going to go pick us up some food and salve for your frostbite."

I stood and grabbed my old jacket, slinging my bag over my shoulder. With one final glance, I left the cabin.

All the way to the village, her face stuck in the front of my mind. When she stared with an empty gaze into the fire, I could see that she was unhappy. I wanted to make everything okay again, but I wasn't sure how, not after that. I would have to show her that she wasn't a burden to me. In fact, she was the complete opposite. I was just going to have to somehow show her.

I always did the best I could when it came to her. We had little, but I had never let that stop me from getting her all the books she desired, or all the flower seeds she wanted for her garden. I showed her how much I loved her through those small acts. I realized that she must not have understood. I didn't just do those things out of obligation, but out of love for her.

There was now a rift between us that had never been there before. It was a rift of misunderstanding, and I wanted to fix it as soon as possible.

Chapter 2

The morning sun warmed my face, and upon reaching the village, I quickly traded for what I needed, giving furs in exchange for food.

If I was going to show her how much she meant to me, then the merchant would be a good start. Perhaps I could find her a nicer gift, jewelry maybe. I had never given her anything like that before. There was no time like the present.

A small bell dinged in the old shop as I entered. When I stepped up to the counter, the merchant eyed me. He seemed, for a moment, uncertain.

"Adric, right?" He looked at me from under his scruffy eyebrows, his finger tapping quietly on the counter. His family were old-timers in the village, just like my own family, and I wasn't surprised he knew who I was. He had to be in his eighties by then, his back hunched with old age.

"Yes, that's me, sir," I answered.

"I was wondering if I could talk to you in the back for a moment. It'll be quick."

"Sure."

He nodded and walked to the back with me close on his heels. His small beady eyes flashed in every direction, and his bony frame almost vanished behind his goods.

I wasn't sure what he could possibly have to tell me, but the way he was acting made me uneasy. I thought, perhaps, it had something to do with trade goods or some drama in town I hadn't heard of yet. It couldn't be anything too serious.

We entered his small office, and he shut the door behind him with a soft click. He turned to me, worry etched in his features.

"Look, son," he took in a deep breath and spoke quietly, not wishing to be overheard. "The boys are getting up to no good again. You know the ones I mean?" We were a small enough village that I knew exactly who he was talking about. I nodded. They were always getting into trouble. I had lived peacefully on the outskirts of the village my whole life, and I tried my best to stay out of their way.

"A friend of mine was down at the pub the other night and apparently there was some chatter," he continued. "There was some talk about someone who lived right in the woods. I guess they saw someone. I don't know much else, but I'm aware of your circumstances with your folks and that you still live out there, continuing in your father's footsteps. I thought I'd let you know. Could be nothing. But it's always good to stick together, us old-timers." He gave a hesitant half-smile.

My family had lived in the village for several generations. Once they had found a spot with plentiful furs to trade, they settled down, and I have lived there ever since.

Whether it was rumor or something more, the news concerned me, especially since those boys had once been my classmates in school. They knew who I was, and one of them, especially, did not think too fondly of me. He struck me as an idiot and a slob, but he had a great deal of charisma, and that made him dangerous.

"Thank you, sir, for the knowledge." I nodded and smiled, trying to be as respectful as I could.

He clasped my shoulder with his worn, still-strong hand and gave me his own warm smile. "Alright, then. You run along." He patted my back and led me to the front of his shop. With a wave, I was off on my way home.

My mind wandered on the long walk back, and I realized I had forgotten to get Calum something, but at least I was bringing her some good food like I had promised. There was always tomorrow, I reasoned.

What the old man said concerned me. It concerned me that those boys were talking about me. It had to be me. There was no one else. I was sure whatever they were plotting wasn't good either. My biggest concern was not for myself, but for what I had hidden back at the cabin, and she was in no way capable of defending herself. I had to find out what they were up to. I made up my mind. I would go tonight to their usual spot and find out.

We spent the rest of the day at home in an uncomfortable silence. She slept the day away, and by the time it was dusk, she was still snoozing, wrapped up in her blanket in front of the fire. It was almost like she was trying to ignore me. I tried not to give in to that thought.

I stoked the fire one last time, then donned my worn cloak, pulling my hood up over my head to cover my face, and, as a precaution, I strapped on my short sword. It was the only weapon I had besides my bow, and I didn't necessarily know how to use it, but it made me feel better to have it just in case. I usually kept it in the back of the closet as I had no need for it.

By the time I was on my way, the day was all hazy and strange. The sun was just setting past the mountains. Everything was gold with only the dark outline of the trees against the gray sky.

The town was alive that evening, unlike the last. The windows were shedding golden firelight and candlelight, and sounds of conversation resonated inside and out on the street. It was not bitterly cold like the other night, either. Spring was coming, and it came fast here. One day it was winter, and the next the snow would be melted with grass emerging. The change could be felt in the air, and everyone was energized.

Once I reached the center of town, I saw even more people. The pub door was wide open, and people of all calibers were coming and going, celebrating the break from the cold. The whole town was a shadow compared to that bright doorway beaming into the night. The two-story townhouses surrounding the square were bathed in the warm glow streaming out. The large stone church across the way stood silent, strong, and regal. A candle burned in each window, warm and welcoming.

I headed toward the heated glow from the pub, my boots scraping against the cobblestones, and I saw exactly what I expected when I entered.

The boys were easy to spot, all obnoxiously loud at the far end of the bar. Lucian was there, and I grimaced. He was in his element, giving out drinks to those he deemed friends but were actually more like followers. Somehow, they saw something in him. Perhaps it was the way he held himself so confidently or the way he clapped each of them on the shoulder and looked them in the eye as if they were all uniquely special to him. He laughed openly and listened intently. He was a boy playing at being a man.

I found my way past the filled tables to the back of the room and watched, my hood still up. A beer was brought, even though I couldn't afford one, and I held it between my hands and simply watched. The fire roared in the fireplace, and the candles were all lit. The moose antlers over the fire made all those who visited aware that they were out in the wilderness. Everyone was laughing and talking, filling the place with warmth and rosy cheeks.

The boys drew my attention once more as they let out a burst of laughter, and I could almost make out what was being said in the crowded room, which was impressive.

"Trust me! I've seen her with my own eyes," Lucian yelled, and his voice filled the room. His eyes were intense as he tried to convince some of his comrades. His words slurred slightly, and the beer in his hand almost sloshed onto the floor. His soft, brown hair kept falling into his eyes, and he was still scrawny, not yet fully formed into an adult.

They snorted and shook their heads, and he gripped his pint harder. His eyes flicked to the closest table to them, and he stalked over. He purposefully placed his pint down on their table, gaining their attention.

"Any of you believe in witches?" He looked into each of their eyes as he leaned forward.

He was smiling, but it didn't seem like a joke. His front teeth were visible and slightly crooked, his boots almost worn through. I didn't see anyone else notice those things. His presence commanded that he be taken seriously, especially those piercing blue eyes of his.

The only response he got, though, were a few shrugs. He scoffed.

"I saw one," he said in a lowered voice, "in this town." He nodded and glanced around the room as if she could be hiding anywhere. There were a few smirks passed around. The drunker ones frowned.

He stepped back from the table and raised his voice, "Has anyone else seen the witch? I've seen her with my own two eyes, casting some kind of spell off in the woods."

By then, he had gathered the attention of most of the room with his shouting, and the room was falling silent as they watched the show.

THE THINGS OF NATURE

"I saw her with my own two eyes, I say! She was disguised, but I saw through it! A real witch!" He pointed up as if to make his point, his eyes wide.

People around the room murmured, and I clenched my hands around my pint. My mind was jumping to all the worst places. It was possible he was talking about Calum. We were some of the only people who lived outside the village. There were maybe one or two others, but they were older and seen often in the village. Calum was no witch, and she certainly did not go out in the woods in the winter. He couldn't be talking about her. He couldn't have seen her. She was at home. After all, there was no such thing as magic or witches. There couldn't possibly be people here who would believe him.

But Lucian was gaining everyone's ears, and his friends came to stand behind him to listen. It made him look even larger with that pack behind him.

"There is a witch that has come," he lowered his voice from a shout, and he spoke with conviction, "and I did see her. I'm sure some of you have seen the signs. Henry!" He pointed to an older man in the crowd. "Your heifer birthed a stillborn just last week, did she not?"

The old man hesitated. "She did, just last month."

"Ha!" Lucian proclaimed and clapped his hands together. "There's proof!"

Several shook their heads. Things like that happened all the time.

Lucian's eyes darted around the room once more. He then pointed toward one of the girls working the bar.

"Lady! Your wee babe is only a month or so, is he not?" Lucian beckoned to her, and, with all eyes focused her way, she blushed and didn't move.

Lucian saw he was not going to get a response, and he leaped over the counter. The girl yelped as he reached down and grabbed a small bundle from where it had been sleeping. He really was putting on a show as his eyes flicked up to the crowd. They were all watching him, waiting to see what he would do. Some almost stood, concerned for the babe.

"This is proof," he spoke in a hush. "All of you, see for yourselves."

He then turned the baby around and held it up for all to see. At first glance, he looked completely normal, but with a closer look, you could see that he had a cleft lip. I felt my mouth twist in disgust at the realization that he was using the baby to fan the flames of superstition and prejudice. Plenty of people were different, and I truly didn't like how Lucian was using this difference to further his own plan.

Angry voices rose in the crowd at the sight, some at Lucian for being so crude, but they also saw it as actual proof of Lucian's claim. They were angry, both with him and at him.

"Look!" he spoke louder. "This innocent babe!" He continued to hold it up for all to see, and the small thing began to cry. The mother rushed in to take him back and Lucian handed him over.

"Listen, all of you!" Lucian commanded them. "I know where the witch is. You just have to follow me. We should kill it now while we have the chance! Before she curses anyone else. We don't need any devil worshippers here!"

A few stood, nodding their heads. There weren't many of them, maybe five, but they were enough. These were the superstitious folk. There was wariness and concern in their eyes. They believed these signs. The firelight flickered across their worn beards and hands, and their eyes were hard. No one was going to stop them.

More stood, drunk and intrigued. They wanted to watch the show.

"Grab what you can!" Lucian spoke, moving forward. "We will need all we have against this witch!"

I was running. I don't remember when I began to run, but I was running, the cold slicing into my lungs.

Calum. All I could think about was Calum. He must have seen her at some point. I had no idea how, but it must have happened. I couldn't think of anyone else it could be. I also couldn't understand why he would do this. Maybe he enjoyed the power he was able to hold over people. Perhaps he was lapping it up like a hungry dog. His grin had certainly said enough. It was the last thing I had seen, and it stuck like glue in my mind.

By the time I reached the cabin, my legs were shaking, and I couldn't breathe. I slammed into the door, and it banged open.

Calum jumped and stared at me in astonishment.

"We have to go! There's no time!" I ran to grab our things, my shaking legs barely making it up the stairs. I didn't know how much time we had, but I knew it wasn't much. They would be coming with their pitchforks and torches, and even though there weren't that many of them, there was only one of me to protect her. Even though I had lived there for a long time, I didn't have any leverage. I had never made any friends because I had done my best to hide Calum away, and even before I had met her, I had normally kept to myself.

A queasy feeling took over as I realized what a mistake it had been for me and Calum to stay alone with no friends to speak of. With no one to help us, I could only imagine what they would do to her.

I grabbed my sack, filling it with clothes for both of us, then ran back down to grab some food. We needed to get out. I couldn't take any chances with her, and I knew the best thing would be to get out of town. That was our best option if they were really coming.

Calum sat at the edge of her cot, her eyes still groggy but concerned. "Adric." Her voice was soft. "What's wrong?"

"There's no time to explain." I grabbed her coat and wrapped it around her. She slowly put it on, and I wrapped my arm around her.

"Are you okay to walk?" I questioned.

She nodded slowly and stepped toward the door. "Yes, yes."

I grabbed the handle, and then we were out, startled by the cold night. I could see Calum's breaths coming out in clouds. She began shivering, her curls bundled around her. The moon was full, and it shone brightly down the path. But there was also another light. It was the warm glow of fire coming toward us. They truly were coming our way. My heart sank at the sight and fear jolted me into action.

"This way." I grabbed her hand, and we headed into the woods. There was nowhere else to go. If we could skirt the village, then we could reach the road leading out of town.

The snow crunched under our feet as we hastened into the darkness. There was no time for me to cover our tracks. It was impossible to run smoothly without more light, and every few steps Calum tripped over something, whether it was a root or stone. It was rough going, and twigs snagged or pulled at our clothes. The woods themselves almost desired to hinder us. The farther we headed the more enclosed I felt, wrapped up in the silence of the forest.

Then there was a soft glow. It rose from behind us and lit our path. For a moment, I thought they were following us, but then I realized that the light was getting bigger and warmer. It was the house. They had lit it on fire. It was burning quickly.

I felt a bloom of anger in my chest for these people and myself for being so helpless and unable to stop them.

With a glance back, I could see the flames licking up toward the night sky. If I hadn't needed to protect Calum, I might have been able to face them and show them that there was no witch. But I was not willing to take those chances. The only thing we could do was move forward. There was no time to stop. We had to continue. Our footprints would be easy enough to follow, and I knew that they would find them quickly.

I gripped Calum's hand harder and pulled her to move faster. Her hand was already cold, and I could see she was trying her best. It wasn't long before we heard shouts, and I knew we were being followed. The chase was on.

The woods seemed endless the longer we ran. Calum was having a hard time keeping up, and it didn't take long for her to begin to slow down, her breath coming in gasps. But we had to hurry. They were hot on our trail.

We had to be passing our village then, skirting around the edge. We were going to have to start turning back so we could find the main road out of town. That was our best shot. I knew the woods well, but only so far.

Then Calum's grip was wrenched from mine. I whipped my head around and skidded with the sudden stop. She had fallen. She picked her shaking hands up off the cold snow, which was sticking to her fingers and face. I grabbed her to help her to her feet. She was so weak. She couldn't go much farther, but we had to keep going. I turned and hefted her onto my back. Coat and all, she was bulky, though still pretty light, a small little thing. She wrapped her arms around my neck, and I held her legs with my arms. My hair was falling into my eyes.

We moved at about the same pace, but at least Calum wasn't going to fall anymore or get any slower. And, at that moment, I was extremely grateful for all of those long hunting trips, the grueling hours climbing, tracking, and running through the wilderness. The muscles I had built up were saving us.

My hope of escape withered as we heard the howl of the first dog, a hunting dog. I almost couldn't believe what I was hearing. It blew my mind that the villagers were pulling out all the stops to catch us. The dogs would only take seconds to reach us.

Then they were there, surrounding us, barking and snarling, showing their reflective white teeth in the moonlight.

"Adric!" Calum clung to me, her arms almost blocking the airways in my neck. She was frightened, terrified, and I could barely catch my breath.

The dogs came closer, trying to gauge us. If I was going to act, then I had to act fast. I kicked, sending snow into the face of the one in front of us. It leaped back and I made a dash. They immediately followed, howling for their masters, nipping at our heels. I kept kicking snow the best that I could, but it was useless as I ran. The dogs merely followed us a few paces back.

The road. We had reached it before I realized it, and I almost tripped up the small embankment. The dirt road stretched true for miles and miles, heading straight for the great capital city of the Central Kingdom—Amartoth.

Wilderness surrounded us, and the road only led to the city or back toward town. It would be even easier for them to spot us there. I felt so dumb. I hadn't thought that far ahead. I hadn't expected dogs.

I started down the road, but the dogs were there, snarling. I was like a trapped deer and I knew my fate. There was also Calum. I gripped her tighter. I was not going to let her go.

I loved her. I loved her with every bone in my body. That had been the secret I had been keeping for so long. It was the secret I had wanted to tell her the other night when I had brought her flowers. That emotion made it easy to turn from my parents' cabin, to turn away from everything. All that mattered to me was her, even if she didn't feel the same way.

Pain soared up my leg, and I stumbled, falling to the ground with a shout. Calum fell beside me. A dog had my ankle in its teeth, and he growled loudly. The others moved forward, and I waved my hands wildly, yelling, trying to get them to back off. Calum grabbed onto my shoulder not knowing what to do and cried out as she saw the dog rip into my ankle.

Chapter 3

Then, one of them squealed, and the one with the iron grip on my ankle let go. I could barely register what was happening as a horse and hooded rider swooped in, the horse kicking. They had burst from the woods on the other side of the road so suddenly it had frightened the dogs, and with a nasty kick from the horse, the first dog went squealing back the way it had come.

The rider whooped and hollered, wavering his arms wildly, appearing larger than life, his cloak billowing behind him. The horse followed his example, and like a crazy pair, they charged through the dogs turning this way and that. It wasn't long before the dogs went careening back through the underbrush toward their masters.

With a quick "Ha!" of triumph, the rider slid off his mount and threw back his hood. He was young, in his late twenties, which was slightly older than me, and a large grin spread across his face, his blue eyes twinkling. The yellow shock of his hair shone in the moonlight, and by the way he held himself with his well-muscled frame and the sword at his side, I could tell he was well-trained and at ease. But there was also some healthy stubble along his jaw, and his clothes were worn as if he hadn't changed in several days. I wasn't sure what to make of him.

"Looked like you two needed some assistance." He held out his hand for Calum, and she hesitantly took it. He pulled her to her feet. She was shivering visibly, and she wrapped her arms around herself. With some effort, I slowly came to stand using my good leg and then wiped the dirt from my hands onto my pants.

"The name is Cassius, by the way, and we better get out of here before they come back." He gestured to his horse.

I finally managed to speak through my surprise. "We really appreciate it. You don't even know us."

He rolled his eyes, giving us a small smile. "I wasn't about to leave you two to play with those dogs." Then, turning to Calum, he gestured toward his horse. "May I?"

She nodded hesitantly again, almost shyly, and I remembered that it had been a significantly long time since she had met someone.

With her nod, he deftly picked her up by the waist and sat her up in the saddle. With a quick glance at my ankle, he frowned. "You better get up there, too."

I hobbled over, and he gave me a boost using my good foot, creating a cradle with his hands for me to step on. I sat right behind the saddle and wrapped my arms around her.

Cassius's face was slightly more serious as he took the reins, and we headed down the road away from the village. He glanced into the woods the way we had come, but there was no movement. We set the pace at a slow trot.

From the wetness of my sock, I could tell I was bleeding in my boot, and with each little jolt, I felt pain shoot up my leg.

Calum shivered before me, her hands clutching the horse's mane. She was small in the saddle, and her dress rode up leaving her legs mostly bare to the cold. I held her as tightly as I could, and it felt good to hold her so close to me—to feel that comfort, to feel like I was shielding her from the cold a little bit.

I kept glancing back the way we had come, waiting for the dogs and men to return, but they didn't. Perhaps they had called it off. Perhaps they had only wanted to chase us out of the village. Or maybe the alcohol had worn off.

Either way, I couldn't believe that people from the village would do this. I couldn't understand why Lucian would do this. These past twenty-four hours were like a tumult swimming through my brain. Our roots and our lives were ripped up so easily. First, our relationship and the fact that I thought I had known her. Then, I had no idea what was going through her head. I had never truly known her, and it scared me. It scared me more than what we had just gone through. It was crazy. We had nothing, just like that. I had no idea where we were supposed to go.

Glancing up at Cassius again, his back to us, I realized his cloak was torn, and his hair was a completely tangled mess on top of his head. It made me wonder where he came from. Certainly not the village. I would have recognized him. Perhaps he was traveling. There were many questions I wished to ask our hero, but I kept my mouth shut. He had saved us after all. I didn't want to appear like I didn't trust his intentions.

He startled me when he spoke. "I spent last night in an abandoned place. It's pretty well hidden, and I have some supplies."

"Thank you," I spoke softly, holding Calum tighter. I could tell that he wanted to ask us questions as well by his glances. But he kept his mouth shut, probably a courtesy since I was doing the same.

Soon after he spoke, we headed off the road and into the woods, and I felt relief for the protection of the trees. A small stream wound its way, and we followed it till we came to an old-looking cabin. It had certainly been abandoned, but it could have been in worse shape. Weeds and vines climbed up the walls, but everything was still intact. A wisp of smoke still rose from the chimney where Cassius had made his fire during the day.

Reaching the door, we came to a stop, and we slowly slid down—or fell off—Cassius's horse. He ushered us inside, and upon passing the threshold, I felt the exhaustion hit me. My muscles were sore from running and carrying our few possessions and Calum. I hastily hobbled over to an old rocking chair and slid down into it, putting my foot out.

THE THINGS OF NATURE

Glancing around, I saw the cabin was a single room. A small bed was in the corner by the fire, and there were two chairs and a table. The floor was dirt, but the atmosphere was cozy. It had to have been a hunting cabin at one time, and as Cassius stoked the fire and threw some more wood on, the place lit up with a warm glow.

"Let me see." Cassius crouched in front of me and deftly unlaced and removed my boot, making me hiss in pain. It wasn't as bloody as I had thought it might be. Though my sock was stained red, it wasn't soaked.

"Give me a second." Cassius stood. "Let me grab some stuff from my pack." Then he went out the door. He was still serious, but not worried.

As a hunter, I also knew the difference between a bad wound and one that could heal without a doctor. This was certainly a quick fix. As long as there was no infection, there would be no problem.

"Are you alright?" Calum's soft voice rose from beside the fire where she had sat on the dirt floor. Her shivering had stopped, but her eyes looked drained.

"I'll live," I answered. "How are you?"

She turned her eyes back to the fire and replied the same—"I'll live."

I could tell she was trying to sound unfazed and teasing, but I knew the experience must have left her shaken. Her entire life was a pile of ashes several miles away.

"I'm so sorry, Calum. I don't know how they found out about you." I wanted to comfort her; I just didn't know how.

"It's not your fault, Adric. It's not like we were living that far from the village. Someone was bound to notice sooner or later. If it's anyone's fault, it's mine."

At that moment Cassius came back in, and the conversation ended. There was still more I wanted to say. I would just have to talk to her later.

Once Cassius cleaned and wrapped my leg, he went back over to the fire and stoked it. "I suggest you two get some rest." He stood straight and pulled his cloak back on.

"Where are you going?" I immediately questioned.

He smirked. "Guard duty. Now get some rest. We can talk in the morning." And with that, he was out again, his sword strapped at his side. I had no doubt he knew how to use it by how confidently he carried himself while wearing it.

I opened my mouth to speak to Calum again, but her eyes were drooping as she stared at the flames. So instead, I said, "Calum, go and take the bed. I'm fine here."

She looked at me quizzically. "But your leg . . ."

I shook my head. "Just take the bed." I spoke more commandingly than I had meant to, but she did as I asked and was soon out cold.

⊹⇌◉⇋⊹

Calum woke in the night, the silence surrounding her. The fire was still bright and burning thanks to Cassius, but Adric was sound asleep.

She watched him breathe softly. His clothes were rumpled and his hair was messy, but his face was relaxed with sleep.

She felt the weight of guilt rest upon her. She had been seen. She should have been more careful. She shouldn't have strayed so closely to the village.

At the same time, when they had turned and seen the cabin burning through the trees, she hadn't felt sad. Strangely, she had felt nothing.

The cabin had been her home for so many years. She had read so many books and cooked so many meals and cleaned each room so many times. But as she watched all of those things burn, she had felt nothing.

If anything, she felt a slight weight lift off her shoulders. When she had climbed that mountain, she had wanted to free Adric to let him live his life. Now that his home was destroyed, she thought it was pointless. They both had nothing and all they had left was each other. Things were different now.

She also realized that she felt free from the chains of what her life had felt like at the cabin. She had been free, but with nowhere else to go, she had felt trapped. Their situation was worse, but at least she wouldn't have to live the same day over and over again. She had done the same things every day, year after year.

She was free. Things would change. They would see new things, find a new home, and hopefully, things would be different. She wasn't sure how, but she hoped they would.

Perhaps she hadn't climbed that mountain just for Adric, but maybe a little bit for herself, too. Maybe she had wanted to free herself from the bonds of the cabin just as much as she had wanted to free Adric so he could live his life. She had been safe there, but it had been stifling.

She closed her eyes once more and fell back into a deep sleep.

⋄⇒◎⇐⋄

When I opened my eyes, there was a soft morning light coming through the dirt-speckled windows. The fire was down to coals, and Calum still slept exactly where she had been when I closed my eyes.

Testing my leg, I could feel that it was sore, but not painful. I was just thankful that Calum was uninjured. And at that moment, I needed fresh air. Our situation was overwhelming. The whole situation made me feel like everything was out of my control. I had always managed to take care of her until then, but now we were both helpless. The night before had made me realize how helpless I truly was. The fact that I was simply relieved at her being uninjured made me feel terrible.

I hobbled outside and sucked in the fresh air. It wasn't as cold as it had been the day before, and the sun was melting the snow. Spring was certainly on its way.

As I suspected, Cassius was sitting outside on a fallen log. I could tell he had shaved, flattened out his hair, and even washed some of his clothes in the stream, probably for Calum's sake. They were still quite damp in different patches, but he didn't seem to mind. He looked like a proper soldier once again, or at least that's what I assumed he was.

Hearing the soft click of the cabin door, he looked up at me and nodded in greeting.

"You hungry?" he questioned, reaching into his pack, which rested at his feet.

"A little." I sat beside him.

He handed me a piece of dried meat and continued to work, whittling a piece of wood with a small knife.

"Thank you, again." I tried to make conversation. I certainly owed him another thank you after what he did for us.

He continued without looking up. "It's what anyone would do. Who were those people anyway, if you don't mind me asking?"

I sighed. "Some people from the village." I didn't want to tell him that they had suspected Calum of being a witch. After the previous day, I had concluded that people were more superstitious than I had originally thought. I was sure Cassius was a decent person, but you could never know for certain how someone would react.

"Hmm." Some major parts were obviously missing from the story, but he didn't press. "Do you have somewhere else to go?" His eyes finally met mine, and I could tell he was genuinely curious. I didn't know how to answer. I hadn't even thought that far ahead.

"No." I sounded deflated even to myself. I had no plan. I spent most of my time in the forest surrounding the village, and the village was the only home I had ever known. Our cabin was gone, but at least I still had Calum.

I could tell by the look in his eyes that he understood. We had nothing and nowhere to go.

He turned back to his whittling without saying anything, and I could tell he was contemplating something. His brow was furrowed and his jaw clenched.

I turned back to eating and felt embarrassed.

After a few minutes of thoughtful silence, he spoke again, "I'll take you."

I looked at him startled. "Where?"

"Toward Amartoth. Not all the way there, but I'll help you through the Dark Forest. You should be able to make it from there."

I had only heard stories of Amartoth and how vibrant and full of power it was. Perhaps we could find a new life for us there. Get a job, find somewhere to live. It was probably the best option we had.

"Thank you." Again, I was genuinely thankful for the offer. "You don't have to do that. You've done enough."

He shook his head. "If you've never traveled through the Dark Forest before it would be good to have a guide. It can be dangerous."

I nodded. He certainly knew what he was talking about more than I did.

At that moment the cabin door creaked open, and Calum emerged, blinking into the sun.

I stood and walked toward her. "Calum, how are you feeling?" I could tell that she was better. She had color back in her cheeks, and she looked well rested. But I asked anyway.

She looked up at me and smiled hesitantly. "I'm feeling good. How's your ankle?"

"It's sore, but I can walk on it."

She looked slightly embarrassed. "I just heard you two talking so I came out."

"Are you hungry?" I questioned.

"Yeah." She smiled. "I'm quite hungry."

I was pleased to see that she was pretty much back to her normal self.

I laughed a little at her admission and led her to sit next to us on the fallen log.

Cassius handed her some more reserves from his bag and smiled at her, saying, "My lady."

She blushed and took the food from him. "Thank you."

Calum began to eat, and I told her the plan. She took a moment to ponder, then finally whispered, "Is it safe there?"

Cassius overheard. He shrugged. "It's as safe as anywhere, love."

I put my arm around her shoulders and squeezed, giving her a reassuring smile.

"Alright," she agreed, nodding, but her eyes were still sad.

I imagined she was thinking about what we lost, and it made me sad, too, depressed even. It was going to be hard for both of us, starting over from scratch. The final reminder of my parents was gone. Everything I was,

was gone. All we had were the clothes and money I had managed to grab.

"We'll be okay." I tried to reassure her and myself.

"It wasn't your fault, Adric." She gave me a sad smile and patted my knee. She must have thought that was what I had been thinking about.

"Are you married?" Cassius's question threw me off guard, and I was startled into silence for a moment.

"What? No, no!" I answered, fumbling over my words.

Calum quickly took her hand off my knee, looking concerned.

"Oh, sorry, an honest mistake." He looked between us for a moment, then with a silent smile to himself, he began to pack his things.

I could understand where his question came from. We had always been close since we had been much younger when we had met. That was the way it had always been, but perhaps, when we were not alone, I would have to think before touching Calum from then on. It was going to be a bit of a change, and I felt sad at the loss, even though it was small. I liked being close to her, just the two of us, comfortably close. It didn't help that I had romantic feelings for her.

Cassius gave a piercing whistle, jerking me from my thoughts. "Time to go," he announced and stood, stretching.

Before I had time to question him on being so loud, his horse trotted out of the underbrush, unbridled and looking wild. It stopped by him and nuzzled his hand as if looking for a treat.

Cassius smiled widely. "There you are." He patted her, then reached into his pocket, but instead of giving it to her, he held it out to Calum. "Here."

"Are you sure?" Calum looked at his outstretched hand.

"It's just a sugar cube," Cassius joked, handing it to her. She took it reluctantly.

"Hold your palm up, hand flat," he instructed.

She did as she was told.

"Her name is Pumpkin. Don't tell anyone."

He smiled as Pumpkin picked up the small cube with her lips, looking very happy, her tail swishing.

"Pumpkin?" I asked, looking at him incredulously.

"Don't tell." He winked, then began to saddle her up.

Turning to Calum, I saw that she was smiling. It was a genuine smile that reached her eyes as she looked at Pumpkin. It hit me then that it had been a long time since I had seen that smile, and it made me sad. I couldn't believe I hadn't noticed before. It made me think back to the night when I had found her on the mountain with no coat. It must be connected, her running away and her unhappiness. Why she had tried to leave was still a mystery to me since her explanation had made no sense. She had spoken as if she had done it *for* me, but I would never want her gone. It would break me.

After running inside and grabbing our things, we clambered onto Pumpkin. I got up first, then Calum climbed in front of me. I wrapped my fingers in the horse's mane and Calum kept hers on the pommel. From what I could tell, it was going to be a long journey. The city of Amartoth was days away. I wasn't sure how many days, but I knew at least a week if not more.

The only thing I could do was hope that once we got there, we could find a place to stay and work. I hoped we could fit in and adapt to that new life. It was going to be a big change for us, and I knew we would always mourn our lost home.

I was angry at the men who had done that to us. I was angry at Lucian, at myself for being unable to stop them, and the whole situation, but there was nothing we could do about it. The only thing we could do was to look forward.

THE THINGS OF NATURE

    Cassius took the reins and led us back toward the main road.

CHAPTER 4

Night couldn't come soon enough. Calum and I were both exhausted and sore from riding all day. Cassius didn't seem to be any worse for the wear. He had walked all day, but he looked used to it. With his sword at his side and a torn cloak over his shoulders, it looked like he belonged out there, like he did that all the time. The moment we reached the main road I had begun to feel uncomfortable in the saddle.

When evening arrived, we pulled off the road and headed into the forest. Once we came to a large enough clearing, we made camp—not that we really had anything to make camp with.

Calum and I practically fell off Pumpkin upon stopping, and Cassius smirked at us. "You'll get used to it."

THE THINGS OF NATURE

We only took a few steps before sitting down. Our legs were so wobbly and sore we couldn't have made it any farther.

At least the day had warmed. Spring was in the air, and the snow had melted. In fact, it was warm enough outside that we would all be sleeping comfortably that night, even if it was on hard ground. No breeze and no sound came from the road, either. We hadn't passed a single soul and that confused me. I would have expected to at least see a merchant or two as it was the only road toward the village, but there had been nothing.

"Cassius, is it normal not to see anyone on the road?" I asked.

He turned from where he was unsaddling Pumpkin. "It's only like this around the time of a shadow moon."

"When the moon is in shadow," I clarified, and he nodded.

"Why is that?" I asked.

"No one travels through the Dark Forest when there's a shadow moon." He spoke as if that was a good enough explanation and obvious.

I repeated my question. "Why?"

Cassius sighed.

"It's more tradition than anything else at this point. There's this superstition. It's just bad luck or something like that, but it's become normal practice since it's been done farther back than anyone can remember."

I looked at him quizzically. "Bad luck?"

He shrugged. "Well, the story is that there's a witch who controls the Dark Forest, and whenever there's a shadow moon, she's able to slip some of her magic out and kidnap people. Totally ridiculous, honestly."

The whole thing sounded silly enough to me. "So, there is no real danger or anything?"

"Bandits sometimes take advantage of such places, but we shouldn't run into them with the shadow moon." He finished untacking Pumpkin and let her go. He then came over and sat a few feet away from me, looking up at the stars.

I thought to myself that it sounded strange for everyone to avoid one place at the same time every month and believe in such a silly story. There must be more to it. I did not believe in silly superstitions. But I also did not wish to be the person to test it out.

"Are you sure it's safe?" I questioned.

He rolled his eyes. "I'm sure. And it's better this way. We won't run into any of your little village friends."

He at least had a point there. I could give him that.

Then Calum's small voice came from my other side. "Maybe we should just wait?"

Cassius smiled a big, reassuring smile. "No need to worry, Princess. You'll be safe with me."

That didn't seem to satisfy her, but she said nothing else and lay back on the ground.

Cassius and I joined her, and I closed my eyes.

The sooner we got through those woods, the sooner we would arrive at the city and our new life. I certainly didn't believe there was any such thing as magic or witches. I had learned there was no such thing when I was young. The hardships of the real world had taught me enough as a child to not believe in miracles or other such silliness. When I was young, there had been hunger during the winter, and I could remember my mother praying. Those had been some of the longest nights. Also, seeing how easily my own village had turned on us because of their superstitions only hardened what I already knew to be true.

Even if we did run into trouble like bandits, we had Cassius, and even though we knew nothing about him, I still felt deep down like I could trust him. The only thing he had shown us so far was kindness.

Whatever the next day would bring, or any day after that, I knew I was at least going to have Calum at my side. Ever since she arrived, she had been a constant in my life, and it made leaving home behind not as hard, for she had become my home. That realization struck me. Calum was everything to me and only when she was gone would I truly be lost. She was my way. She gave me a reason to keep going. She was my sun and I merely spun around her in orbit.

―⁂―

When we woke, frost covered the ground, and it delicately sparkled with the rays of sun that snuck through the branches of the trees. It was a perfect morning.

We headed off almost immediately, only eating a small bite for breakfast.

Cassius informed us that we would be reaching the Dark Forest that evening, and I felt only the littlest bit of concern. We were all going to be fine. Everything was going to be fine. It was just a wood after all. I'd been uneasy about the whole idea, but after sleeping on it, and having the sun shining on us, I felt much better.

I ended up walking much more than the previous day. My ankle was only sore, and when it got too bad, Calum and I would trade places on Pumpkin.

It was easier going that day, especially since I got to stretch my legs.

We tried to make some small talk, but Cassius never said anything about himself. We ended up telling him more about ourselves, like how we had lived before and what I did for a living.

When I mentioned my trapping and hunting, he gave a nod of appreciation. "That will certainly come in useful. There are some good jobs in the city for those with your skill set. You'd be surprised."

When it came to Calum, he was always very cordial, making a joke here or there to make her smile. He was really the perfect gentleman, and that made me wonder again where he had come from and what he had been through. He was highly skilled but also alone. It was strange.

When we crested the next hill, I saw it. Stretching out below us was a wood that was darker and thicker than where we had previously traveled. The trees were much older and gnarled, and their shadows were much more pronounced. Besides the road, which cut a slight path through, there was no break in the density. The leaves were also budding there as if spring had struck a month sooner. The line between the regular wilderness and the Dark Forest was also quite pronounced as if there were a barrier between the two.

"Here we are," Cassius said.

"It's so old," Calum whispered, and Cassius nodded.

"Stick to the road. If you see anything in the wood, ignore it. Just in case. We'll be perfectly fine." Cassius stood a little taller and a little prouder. He was prepared for anything. It was like he was on the verge of excitement.

I, on the other hand, was not.

We headed down the hill, and upon reaching the trees, I thought it was becoming quieter as if the dense trunks prohibited sound from traveling. The trees were even more wrinkled up close as if they were a century old. No human had ever cut a tree down in that forest or cleared the land. It was all untouched.

It also felt warmer there. Little wind made its way through.

We stayed silent as we traveled, not that it would have mattered if we had spoken. It just felt like the right thing to do in a place like that.

I found myself walking closer to Calum where she sat on Pumpkin. It felt safer to keep her only a few inches from myself. It was a comfort in that quiet place. She had always provided that kind of comfort for me.

We stayed like that for most of the day, quiet and somewhat alert, our boots crunching on the dirt the only sound. We passed nobody, as expected, and it made me feel even more that we were alone in the wilderness.

"What's that?" Calum was suddenly alert, her eyes darting across the forest to our left.

"What?" Cassius came to a halt and looked in the direction she was looking.

I saw nothing.

"Do you hear that?" she whispered.

"I don't hear anything, Calum," I responded, looking at her as she sat stone-still.

Cassius glanced at me, and I could see he was concerned. His blue eyes were sharp. "We should keep going."

He was about to nudge Pumpkin to walk again, but Calum shouted, "STOP!"

She startled me so badly I jumped, and I couldn't stop her as she leaped off Pumpkin. Then she ran, and I realized too late I was standing on the wrong side of Pumpkin and couldn't grab her. Cassius made a valiant lunge backward and tripped, and by then, it was too late. She was off the road before I could suck in another breath.

"Calum!" I yelled. Then I was running too. The old leaves crunched under my boots as I hurled after her, dodging trunks. I could just see flashes of her curly hair bouncing in front of me.

Then it was over as quickly as it had begun.

THE THINGS OF NATURE

I caught up to her and grabbed her arm. "Calum! What are you doing?" My chest rose and fell with the sudden excitement, and my eyes followed to where she was staring.

There was a small fox, and it had its teeth bared. It stared at us, and I was wondering why it was not running away until I saw that it was trapped. Its back leg was bloody and mangled from where it was held in an iron grip. The creature was obviously in a lot of pain as it growled at us half-heartedly.

"Just leave it, Calum." I tugged on her arm to pull her away, but she stood firm.

"No." Her voice was hard. I had never heard her be so commanding before.

Then Cassius was beside me. "We need to get back to the road. Now. This isn't right."

"This happens when you're hunting, Calum; it's just life." I tugged again. There was no response.

Instead, she moved forward, very slowly, reaching out her hand. The fox only had eyes for her by then as it snarled.

"Calum, come on!" That time I pulled harder, but she ripped her arm away and turned on me.

"Stop it! Just stop it!" She was so angry her lip was trembling, and I realized that her anger was directed at me. I stared at her in shock. Her cheeks were flushed, and her eyes almost watery as she turned back to the fox. She moved closer, and I said nothing. She knew what she was doing was dangerous, and it wouldn't end well.

She reached out her hand and inch by inch, she slowly approached the fox. It stared at her, waiting for her hand to get closer. Then Calum got down on her knees, so she was level with it, and the fox bared its teeth at her, not growling any more. I watched in stunned silence as her hand came in biting distance and the fox didn't move. They stared into each other's eyes as if they were staring into each other's hearts.

She came around behind it and reached for its leg. The fox did nothing but watch. She grabbed either side of the iron teeth and pulled. The iron jaws opened, and the fox pulled its leg loose, then it was gone, darting into the forest with barely a sound.

Calum released the jaws with a loud snap then shakily stood up. Her eyes met mine and there was still some anger there, and with her curls frizzy, she looked like an angry sprite of the forest. She was defiant, and I had never seen her so strong-willed before.

Without a word, she walked past me, back the way we had come. I slowly turned and followed her, Cassius next to me with Pumpkin's reins still in his hand. He looked between us and kept his mouth shut. He was as startled by the whole encounter as I was. I had no idea what had just happened. Perhaps the fox had lost so much blood it had lost its strength to retaliate, but it hadn't looked that way. She had somehow communicated to a wild animal through her eyes that she was harmless. I knew that if I had tried the same, I would have gotten bit.

We walked in silence back toward the road. When we reached the point where I thought we would be coming upon it, I scanned the dense forest. I couldn't see it yet, and

I felt my palms begin to get sweaty. It was fine. We had just run a little farther than I had thought.

We kept walking, and then walked some more.

Cassius came to a halt and so did Calum and I. We both looked at him.

"We should have reached the road by now." His voice was matter-of-fact. There was no room for argument. He was sure.

"Maybe we turned the wrong way?" I asked hesitantly. My palms were definitely sweating and I felt panic rising inside of me.

Cassius looked around for a moment then turned around. "Let's head back to the trap. We should be able to track our steps from there."

We turned and headed back.

I thought it would be easier to track our path through the old leaves, but it was harder than expected, and soon I wasn't sure where we had stepped or if we were following our path at all. I was good at tracking. It was my job, but all the signs were fading and disappearing before me.

We kept walking, being more careful. We should see the trap any second. It never appeared. We kept walking, then walked some more. It was as if none of us wanted to confirm what we were all thinking, so we kept walking. We were lost.

Chapter 5

Calum finally spoke. "I think we're lost." She looked at Cassius, hoping he would have some answers, but he had none.

He stopped and sighed. "We should stop walking. We aren't going to get anywhere like this."

The wood looked to me the same as it had before, like it never changed. We hadn't come across any body of water or stream. It was just an endless stretch of trees and dead leaves.

The sun was setting, and it was getting harder and harder to see. Calum and I sat on the ground, tired from the long day.

Cassius unpacked Pumpkin. "We'll stay here for the night. In the morning, I'll climb one of these trees and see if I can see the road."

Calum and I sat without reply. He didn't seem as disturbed by the whole situation as we were.

The night was warm, and there was no breeze. My mind began to wander as I lay down. As a skilled tracker and hunter, I felt there was no reason why we should be lost. I was sure Cassius was just as skilled as I was. But we had all somehow gotten turned around. It made no sense. We hadn't run that far from the road in the first place. The only thing that made sense to me was some kind of foul play being involved. As far as I knew, there was no such thing as magic. The only other explanation was bandits. That made even less sense.

It was finally quiet as we all lay on the leaves, trying to fall asleep. Then Calum whispered, "Adric."

She poked my arm, and I opened my eyes to look over at her. There were leaves stuck in her hair and her cheeks were rosy with sleep.

"What?" I whispered back.

"I think I see something." She looked behind us through the trees.

I turned in the direction she was looking and saw a faint glow. There had to be some kind of light, a fire perhaps, in the distance.

"Cassius." I rolled over and nudged his foot with my own.

"What?" he mumbled, already half asleep.

"Look." I pointed in the direction of the light, and he slowly sat up, squinting his eyes at the darkness. I could tell he saw what we saw as he got to his knees for a better look.

"We're not alone," he whispered. Then he grabbed his sword from where it lay at his side. Leaves stuck to his cape as he slung our things over Pumpkin.

"Do you think they could help us?" I whispered, coming to stand by his side.

"I doubt it," he whispered back. "We should be ready to run."

Then, reaching to his belt, he pulled out a dagger. The moon reflected the surface with a deadly shine, and he flipped it deftly in his hand so he was holding its point. He slapped the handle into my hand.

"Are you serious?" I whispered as loudly as I could.

"Just in case," he muttered. Then, tying his sword and sheath back to his belt, he pulled the blade out and it left its hold with a soft *shing*. It was longer and deadlier than I had expected, out in the open. I found myself taking a step back without realizing it. I had never been in a fight of any kind, and I had never seen such a deadly weapon up close before. My dinky sword from home was nothing in comparison.

"Here." Cassius handed Calum the reins. "Follow behind us, and don't lose sight of us."

She nodded and gripped the leather straps, her face determined.

"Come on." He motioned for me to follow, and I did, trying to mimic his stealth.

We neared the glow as quietly as we could. It grew brighter until we could see a fire crackling away, and as we stepped out from behind the trees, we saw that nobody was there. Cassius looked around in confusion, his sword lowering toward the ground. I felt immediate relief that I wasn't going to have to use the dagger.

"Do you think it's a trick?" I spoke softly.

"I don't know." He began to walk his way around the fire, keeping near the trees as he investigated. I stayed where I was, not wanting to get in the way.

I felt something sharp on my neck and froze.

"Don't move." A low voice spoke from behind me, and I realized a sword was at my throat, cold and sharp. I let the dagger fall from my hands to the forest floor. It made almost no sound as the leaves cushioned its fall.

Then, there was a loud clang ripping through the darkness as metal hit metal. As I heard the shout, I knew it was Cassius. Sword hit sword, and he was backed closer to the fire, stepping where I could see him. There were two of them, throwing themselves at Cassius with blades out. It was almost like a dance as they twirled, ducked, and sliced through the air, cloaks flying.

"STOP!" The man behind me yelled, and I flinched at how loud his voice was in my ear.

Cassius turned to look and immediately began to put his hands up in surrender, his hair ruffled.

"Don't hurt him. There's no need to hurt him." Cassius spoke calmly as if to a spooked animal and very slowly crouched down to place his sword on the ground. His chest was rising and falling with the exertion. One of the others grabbed it.

"Who are you? How did you find us?" The voice behind us was commanding, unshaken.

"We're just lost," Cassius replied. "Do you know how to get to the road from here? We'll leave you be. Just point us in the right direction."

The three men hesitated, and I could see them looking at each other in silent communication. I could get a better look at them then, and I could see that they were not much older than us, maybe a few years. But they were unclean and unshaven, which seemed to put many years on them. Their clothes were covered in dirt and had multiple holes. Their hair was hastily chopped out of their eyes with something that was definitely not scissors. They had been out there for a long time I could tell. It was like they had crawled out of the earth, ragged and torn. I saw that they also had bandages, covering wounds.

The one standing beside Cassius spoke. He was lean like a stick and at least a foot taller.

"If you have truly lost the road, then you will never find it again." His voice not as deep as the one behind me.

"Sebastian, is that you?" Cassius whirled around and stared at the tall man beside him, evidently recognizing the voice.

The man looked at him in confusion. "And you are?"

"Cassius." He sighed out a large breath. I wondered if that was relief in his voice.

The man who had to be Sebastian stared at Cassius, his eyes slowly widening in awe.

"Cassius," he whispered, then looked around. "How the hell did you find us?"

"I don't know. It's a shadow moon. We were on the road and then we got lost . . ." he stammered.

"That's what happened to us," the voice behind me said, and he lowered his sword.

I took a few steps away from him and turned around to look at him. He was stocky and well-muscled, shorter than I expected. His brown hair was a mess and just touched his eyelashes. He looked slightly more well-kept than the others.

"Wait," I finally said. "How long have you been here?"

His eyes looked hard into mine, and when he spoke, I could tell that they had given up. "Five years."

Astonished, I yelled, "FIVE YEARS?"

He nodded, whispering, "I'm sorry." It was a statement of finality. I could tell he felt sorry for us and our new fate. Telling us such a thing was hard. If they had been in these woods for five years and had never gotten out, then there was no hope for us. We were stuck there, like them.

"I'm Damian," he added.

"I'm Sebastian, as you now know." The man next to Cassius gave a small mock bow and smiled.

The third finally spoke, his voice soft, his eyes hard and unforgiving. "Anthony."

"Sterling." A fourth emerged from the shadows, startling me. My heart almost skipped a beat at his size. His large sword was strapped across his back and his hair was bright blond, almost white. I had never seen hair like that before. He was the biggest of the four and his jaw lines were sharp.

"Adric?" Calum's soft voice came from the woods, questioning.

"It's safe, Calum. You can come out," I called and she stepped forward, Pumpkin's reins still in her hands.

"Heyyyyyyy, Pumpkin!" Sebastian smiled a wide smile and sauntered over.

The other three looked at Calum with widened eyes. Anthony looked sorrowful, and the others turned from Calum to him, concerned. He actually looked devastated, but then he turned around and walked away. I had no idea what had just happened.

"Ignore him, guys." Sebastian smiled and took Pumpkin's reins. "Come have a seat."

We all moved and sat down by the fire. It was nice and warm, and with no breeze, there was no bad seat. Calum sat close beside me and Damian sat on my other side.

"Is he alright?" Calum asked Damian gently.

"Yeah, seeing you was probably a little rough on him. You see, he had a girl back in the city. Young love and all that. He never even got to tell her goodbye. We didn't know we weren't going to be coming home. But the worst part"—he lowered his voice—"is that she was sick, really sick. He never told us much, but we kind of figured out she was dying."

Calum looked at him mournfully, wrapping her arms around herself. "I'm so sorry."

Cassius gave her a soft smile. "No need to worry, love. It's hard not knowing, I imagine, after all this time. All he really wants is to go home to her."

Sebastian spoke from across the fire. "He's pretty good at moping, that one. You'll get used to it." He chuckled.

Next to him, Sterling had taken a rabbit from his sack and was cleaning it. I assumed that was their supper. Calum didn't look as he cleaned it.

Cassius spoke up. "We still have some rations if you guys are interested." They all looked up at him quickly, looking hopeful. He was all smiles, very pleased at finding his friends, even if we were stuck there. It made sense why he hadn't been so sorrowful about getting trapped when we first arrived or worried about entering the Dark Forest. He had been hoping to find his friends. He added with a laugh, "I thought you might be interested in some biscuits after living in the wilderness for so long."

Sebastian bolted to his feet and put his hand over his heart looking forlorn. "I deserve all the biscuits, Cassius. You remember how I have always been a brother to you?"

"Sit down, Sebastian." Sterling rolled his eyes. His voice was deep like Damian's, but he had an accent, harsh with strong consonants. I had heard that those from the south had sun-kissed hair. Perhaps he was one of them. It was almost difficult to describe him. He was lean and looked fast, but sitting with the others he was the largest. It was a strange combination.

"You all get *one*." Cassius opened his bag and threw a biscuit to each.

Sebastian sat back down with a sigh.

I had so many questions to ask all of them, but there was one question I needed to ask above the rest. I looked at Cassius.

"How do you and Sebastian know each other?" I looked between them waiting for an answer. So far, I still knew nothing about Cassius, and I was beginning to wonder if it was deliberate.

Like I suspected, Sebastian was the one to answer.

"We're both royal soldiers of Amartoth—in the same legion and everything. We're practically brothers if I'm being honest."

I frowned at Cassius. "You didn't tell me you were a soldier." There had to be some kind of explanation for why he hadn't said anything before. If he had told us, we probably would have been quicker to trust him. It wasn't like there was anything wrong with being a soldier. I didn't get why he would keep it quiet. I had suspected it from his clothes, but it was nice to finally know.

He sighed and stared into the fire, ripping apart a dead leaf between his fingers. "We *were* soldiers." He emphasized that one word.

I could see Sebastian pause, his eyes trying to read Cassius's face. "What do you mean?" he almost whispered.

"When you never came home, Captain thought it was deliberate. He thought you guys had deserted."

Sebastian sucked in a breath and anger entered his eyes. "Anyone who knows us knows that isn't true. Anthony would never just leave his girl. I would never leave my family. Damian is the most loyal person I've ever met!" He ran his fingers through his hair violently.

Cassius bowed his head. "I know. That's why I went looking for you. I'm a deserter, too, now."

There was quiet around the fire, and no one looked at each other.

"I always knew Captain was an ass, but this?" Damian shook his head. "He never really cared to get to know us in the first place."

It made sense then why Cassius had told us nothing. He was embarrassed, a deserter. In my mind, caring for friends and worrying for them was a good enough reason to desert his post. The only reason they wouldn't come home was if they were in terrible danger. He knew his friends and the whole situation must have hurt him deeply.

Sterling skewered the clean rabbit and put it over the fire to cook.

After that, we only shared some small talk. I explained where Calum and I were from and how we had run into Cassius. They also all agreed that going to the city was still the best option for us. They even said that if we all were ever able to get out of that mess, they would go with us. After all, they wanted to go home.

Anthony also finally emerged when the food was ready with two new rabbits strung over his shoulder. The conversations died down with his presence. Everything was much more serious around him, darker. It was as if he radiated anger at the world, and it touched everyone nearby.

When we finally lay down to sleep, Damian and Cassius took the first watch. As I lay beside Calum, I could see the two of them talking in whispers, heads bent close together. I was sure there would be more discussion in the morning. They probably knew way more about this place than they had told us. Since they had been there for years, I knew that they would have all the answers. I needed to be patient. We had all the time in the world, after all.

But still, my mind spun. I wondered if we were truly alone in this forest. Perhaps there were other people stuck here. I wondered if there were walls to this trap or if we could keep walking straight forever.

Turning my head, my eyes slid to Calum. She lay on her back, her hands behind her head. She stared up at the leaf canopy and the light of the dying fire reflected off her pupils. She looked completely relaxed, even though we were lost in the unknown.

I couldn't help myself. I reached out and slipped her hair behind her ear. I had always loved her wild curls. They were the opposite of her. She was the gentlest person I knew and seeing her hair gone wild had always made me smile.

She turned her head toward mine, and her eyes became sad.

I rolled onto my stomach and leaned forward on my elbows. "You okay?" I whispered.

She swallowed. "I'm sorry about earlier, Adric. If I had just stayed on the road, then we wouldn't be in this mess." Her eyes were full of guilt.

I shook my head. "It was a trap. How could you have known? None of this really makes any sense, anyway." I took her hand and squeezed it, trying to reassure her. "All I care about is that we are together."

It was true. As long as I was with her, then I didn't care where we were. She was, indeed, my home. If only I could convince her of that.

"Thank you, Adric." She closed her eyes, the soft smile still on her lips.

She didn't let go of my hand, and I was thankful for that. I would hold her hand all night if she let me, and more than anything, with the two of us so close, I wanted to give her a soft kiss on the cheek. The light of the fire made her skin shine like gold, and her cheeks were warmed with the chill in the air. But I refrained and closed my eyes instead. Sleep came quickly.

CHAPTER 6

The next morning, I woke to the sound of low talking. Sitting up, I watched as Sebastian walked around the fire shaking everyone awake as he passed. There was some mumbling, but soon everyone was stretching and rising.

The day had just barely begun, the light still hazy as if the sun were about to rise over the horizon.

When Sebastian crouched beside me to pour water over the fire, I questioned him. "What's the rush?" I imagined we had all the time in the world and nowhere to go.

He glanced at the others, brushing leaves off and gathering their things.

"With the sun up, we have to move," he explained, and then stood, leaving me to wonder what he meant.

I spotted Calum scratching behind Pumpkin's ear and headed in her direction.

"How are you doing?" I asked when I was beside her.

"Much better." She looked up into my eyes. "It was really nice what you said last night."

I smiled warmly in return. "I meant it, Calum. I don't care if we end up on the other side of the world. We're together, so it doesn't matter."

She let out a soft laugh and gave me a big smile. "Well, that's good 'cause I guess you're stuck with me forever now."

"Let's go!" Damian patted me on the back as he walked past, and I saw that the others were beginning to walk off.

"I guess we're at the back of the line," I joked to Calum, and we began following the others.

"Adric?" She pulled my attention again as we walked together.

"Yeah?" I smiled down at her.

Her face broke out into a big grin. "It's like we're on a real-life adventure, you know? Just like I read in all the books back home."

I laughed at that. "I suppose we are, just a little more boring."

She playfully jabbed me with her elbow. "I don't think it's boring."

"Maybe in five years." I patted her on the shoulder, and she rolled her eyes, but her grin remained. It was nice to see her in such a good mood, like the morning had refreshed her.

We walked and walked and walked some more. Nothing changed, and soon we were both tired as the others never let up. I guessed that was what you did to pass the time when there was nothing else to do. I thought a sit-down once in a while would be nice.

In the later afternoon, I found myself walking next to Cassius, and I thought he might know since he talked to Damian often.

"Cassius, why are we walking so much? It's not like we're going anywhere."

He gave me a side glance. "They haven't talked about it too much, but apparently, there's something out there."

My insides immediately became uneasy. Perhaps it would be an exciting adventure after all.

"What do you mean?" I asked.

He glanced over to see if Calum was in hearing distance and when he saw she wasn't, he whispered, "I'm not sure, like an animal or something. It follows everyone so they have to keep moving."

"That's terrifying," I responded. "What's it look like?"

"No idea. But apparently, with Sterling here there's not much to worry about as long as we keep moving."

"What do you mean?" I asked again.

"Well, apparently, he's a trained warrior from the city Persus. It's in the south. They are known for their skill."

"Well, how did he end up here?" I looked in front of us at Sterling, who looked menacing with the giant sword strapped over his shoulder. Other than that, he looked as if he were going for an unhurried evening stroll in the woods.

"Damian said they ran into him shortly after falling into the trap," Cassius answered.

We fell into silence after that, and I found myself staring at Sterling's back as we continued to walk. He fascinated me. He was from a whole different world, a different kingdom. He probably spoke a different language, and who knew how long he had been trapped.

Soon, I could hear something ahead. Running water. A small brook trickled through the wood, small enough you could jump over it in one easy leap.

"Time to refill." Sebastian waved us over as the others splashed water on their faces and we did the same. The water was icy cold, and it felt amazing after walking for so long. We refilled our water supply, and to my surprise, we sat and ate a quick meal. It felt great to sit. I even rolled up my sleeves as the warm sun hit us.

The rest of the day we continued as before, and evening came. The sun was setting, causing the clouds to light in soft pinks and purples. We slowed, trying to scout out a good spot for the night when we heard a rustling of leaves to our left. The guys in the front came to a sudden halt and stared off into the trees. We followed their example and stood like silent statues, frozen in place. A minute passed, but it felt like a century. Then, the noise came again, a soft rustling of leaves far enough away we couldn't see what it was through the trees. The woods were also darkening enough that it was becoming impossible to tell what was shadow and what was not.

Sterling was the first to move. He stepped toward the sound and slowly reached over his shoulder and pulled out his sword. His back muscles tensed with the movement as if he were ready to spring into action, and I felt a little bit of relief. He looked completely impenetrable; a warrior unafraid of anything.

Then the rustling was closer and more to the right. The others pulled out their own swords and began to form something like a circle around us. It was impossible to tell what it was, or if there was more than one of whatever it was.

I reached out and held Calum close to me. Her small hand wrapped around my arm as we looked into the darkness.

The rustling of leaves faded to farther away, and farther away again.

Sterling put his sword away with a quick motion. "The sun has set."

"That was close," Damian whispered as he put his own sword away.

"With more of us, we must be easier to track," Sebastian said simply.

"What was that?" I couldn't help but ask. There was still a slight tremble in my voice. It was one thing to fear some dogs or some men. It was something completely different to fear the unknown.

Damian sighed. "It's hard to explain."

I was a little annoyed with his answer. I was sure they could tell us. I wanted to know, and I was sure they had run into it a few times. "Why?"

Anthony spoke up. "It's just hard to see. No one has gotten a good look at it." He struggled for words as he tried to explain. "You know, it's fast, and it's always covered in shadows."

I swallowed. "How many times have you been attacked?"

"A few times a month if we are lucky," he answered. "But it might be more frequent now, like Sebastian said."

So, that was our fate, running away from something we couldn't see, all day, every day. I could feel the depression and the aggravation beginning to seep through my bones.

Calum squeezed my hand, and I looked down into her eyes. "We'll be okay." She gave me a reassuring smile, and I felt those previous emotions leave me in a rush. A simple tiredness took their place.

"We will," I answered, and we helped the others to make camp.

Sterling left, and I assumed he was going out to hunt. The rest of us sat around our slowly growing fire.

When there was a lull of silence, Anthony spoke up. "Would you like to know how we got stuck here?"

I could tell the question was pointed at me and Calum so I answered, "How?"

I could see he was aggravated, and his anger was only lightly dampened.

"Here we go again," Sebastian whispered just loud enough that I could hear him on my right.

"It was some farmer's feud over some stolen hay. Some stupid stolen hay." He threw the leaf he had been twisting in his hands into the fire. I could tell where his anger was coming from.

"The three of us were sent there by our lieutenant to fix their squabbling on the other side of the Dark Forest. We believed it was so dumb; we wanted to get it over with as quickly as possible. So, we headed through the Dark Forest during the shadow moon. It was dumb, all of it so dumb. We didn't listen to what any of the locals told us. It is out of stupidity that we are here, utter stupidity. Isn't it ironic, all we wanted to do was get home faster to our families, and now we are here?"

"As you can guess, we never even reached the farming village," Sebastian cut in. He was definitely done with Anthony's moping. It annoyed him, as much as Sebastian probably annoyed Anthony. They were both trapped, and they were both dealing with that anger in different ways. Anthony stewed in it, while Sebastian laughed it off.

"I'm sorry, Anthony." Calum's calming voice rose above the crackling of the fire, and I looked over at her in surprise. Anthony was immediately subdued and calmed by her soft voice and her words.

"The same thing happened to us," Cassius spoke. "We saw something in the forest and were led off the road. It's a pretty good trap. It's not anyone's fault."

"We were lured by a damsel in distress, though." Sebastian smiled. "We could hear her in the forest, but we never found her. She was an illusion of some kind."

"Anthony was the first one off the road. You should have seen him go," Damian replied and they all chuckled.

"Just like Anthony to save a female in distress," Sebastian cooed. They all laughed while Anthony rolled his eyes. Just like that, the situation was diffused.

After that, there was only small talk. Sterling came back with another rabbit, and the night turned exactly into the night before. With some side discussion, I found out that everyone knew as much about Sterling as I did, which was the bare minimum. Although, they did know he spoke another language as he sometimes talked in his sleep. But that was all they had discovered.

That night, I took Calum's hand again, and she squeezed my fingers in return. It was comforting more than anything, and we stared up at the stars for a while together before we fell asleep.

I woke instantly to a soft growl permeating through the woods. The sound was low and made me think of thunder. The others were up immediately, just as I was, eyes alert. The sun was coming up over the horizon.

"It's early," Sebastian hissed, and no one moved.

After only a short pause, Damian muttered, "Let's go."

Everyone moved at once, grabbing their things and throwing them all over Pumpkin's back. We didn't even pause long enough to douse the dead fire that still smoked forlornly.

"Go, go!" Damian whispered as loudly as he could, and we all ran as quietly as we were able through the forest.

Cassius grabbed Pumpkin, and I took Calum's hand as we ran, almost tiptoeing between the trees. Sterling took the rear, his sword out and eyes darting back and forth.

Then, out of the corner of my eye, I thought I saw a flicker of movement. When I turned, there was nothing there.

"Sterling," I hissed and pointed to the left where I had seen the movement. He turned to look, but it was gone as quickly as it had come. While we both stared to the left there was another movement, and that time it was from behind us. Sterling saw it the same time I did and we both turned. That time, I caught a glimpse of it.

It was darkness. With the sun still coming up over the horizon, the early morning light was still dim, but it was close enough that we could see it. It was just its back end, but that was enough for me.

"Behind!" Sterling shouted and everyone broke into a sprint.

I clenched Calum's hand harder in my own; we were running, not caring if we were loud or not. I couldn't get the image out of my head. There had been some kind of tail and claws, but it had been so fast. The only thing I knew for certain was that it was dark, perhaps made from darkness. It was as if night leached from its unnatural skin, and as it moved, shadows simmered in its wake before dissipating into the air.

We could hear it behind us. It was as if it were racing, zigzagging back and forth behind us. It could have caught up with us in an instant, but maybe it was testing us out, looking for the weakest one in the pack. That was what most predators did.

It felt like we were getting nowhere even with the trees zipping by us. Everything looked the same. My lungs were having a harder and harder time gasping for air as the chase continued. I even had to pull Calum along as she began to fall behind with exhaustion.

It must have sensed that we were losing momentum because it was suddenly in front of us. No ... it was running around us in large circles. It moved so fast I couldn't tell where it was at any given second.

We all came to a screeching halt, all of us panting and winded. The others drew their swords and formed a circle with me and Calum in the middle with Pumpkin.

"Here we go." Damian panted, and I realized that they had done it all before. How many times, I wasn't sure, but it was probably quite a few. Their circle tightened, their backs closing in on us as the thing ran faster and faster around us.

"I saw something." Calum somehow squeezed my hand tighter.

"Do you still see it?" I asked, following the direction she was looking. I saw nothing. I looked back at her and then back at the woods, but still nothing.

"I think it's a ... door." Her eyes squinted to get a better look.

"What do you mean, a door?" Damian turned his head to look over his shoulder at Calum.

She had the others' full attention as well. I could see them stilling slightly, listening to the conversation.

"Yes, yes; it's a door!" She became more and more certain the longer she looked, and her eyes widened.

"Are you sure?" Anthony asked firmly, his voice hard.

"Yes!"

"Where?" he asked, and she pointed, straight ahead.

Sebastian spoke up. "We've never seen a door before."

But everyone's attention turned back to the beast as it flew past in a dark blur, right in front of Sterling. He swore, and I guess he blocked whatever the thing had been aiming for since he seemed unharmed.

Then the thing struck again, flashing in its speed across the forest floor. Cassius yelled out in pain, and I turned, eyes wide, to see a big scratch down his arm. Blood flowed freely down his arm and down his sword. Calum let out a scream at the sight.

I instinctively looked at Damian for what to do next. He was the most leader-like figure in the group. If we could survive this thing then I would be able to tell from the expression on his face. All I could see was that he was thinking fast, his eyes darting around. He was weighing our options.

With his eyes finally fixed on Calum, he spoke to her. "Bring us to the door."

She nodded, her eyes turning forward with determination. She then pushed at Anthony's back, urging him to move forward. The circle moved with them, and we became a slow circle of bodies, shuffling through the leaves. The beast backed off, probably unsure of what was happening.

THE THINGS OF NATURE

I couldn't see anything as we neared the supposed door, and when Calum came to a stop, the rest of us stood there, seeing nothing at all.

"Where is it?" Sebastian looked around in confusion, voicing what all of us were thinking.

"It's right there! Right in front of us!" She pointed, and turning to look at each of us, it was her turn to look confused as she realized that none of us saw anything.

"I'm not lying! It's right there!" She kept pointing, and when none of us reacted, she reached past Anthony, and her hand grabbed something we couldn't see. She twisted her wrist like she was turning a doorknob and then she pushed. A doorway appeared as something invisible swung open.

And there was the road, as clear as day. Everyone saw it at the same time, crying out, yelling, swearing.

Then Damian was yelling, "Go! Go!"

Everyone stumbled through the opening onto the road. I turned just in time to watch Calum close the opening, slamming it shut, and it was invisible once more.

There was a moment of silence during which all I could hear was everyone panting, staring in utter amazement at the road and at each other. It was as if the world stood absolutely still for that moment while everyone processed where we were.

Then Sebastian whooped so loud I jumped and watched as he fell to his knee. He placed both hands on the road and slowly fell forward till his forehead touched the dirt.

"It's real! Damian, it's real!" he crowed, and Damian sheathed his sword. He ran up to where Sebastian was on the ground and joined him, picking up a fistful of road dust in his hand, then let it slip through his fingers. "It is real. Sebastian!" He clapped Sebastian hard on the back.

"Let's go!" Anthony stepped forward and stared down the road into the distance. When he turned back to everyone his eyes were dancing. "Let's go home."

There was more whooping as they scrambled to their feet.

A moan rose above the noise, and we all turned to Cassius. He had his arm clutched to his stomach, his face pale. He looked like he was about to pass out.

Damian was the first to act. He cursed, then reached into his bag for a makeshift bandage. While he wrapped Cassius's arm, I looked over at Sterling. He hadn't spoken a word yet. He just stared at the road as if he wasn't sure if it was real or not. He was more cautious than the others.

Sebastian turned to Calum and drew my attention away.

"Calum!" Sebastian grinned, then gave her the biggest hug I had ever seen. I was worried for a moment he might suffocate her, but he let her go.

"How did you do that?" he questioned, but Calum looked as amazed as he did.

"I . . . I don't know."

For the first time, I saw a soft grin on Anthony's lips. "You did it. That's all that matters." With that smile, his features looked less angry. He looked lighter on his feet as if the dark cloud had rolled away. He was finally going to see his girl again.

He also approached Calum. "Thank you." He took her hand in his and squeezed it with a smile. The gratitude in his eyes was almost overwhelming.

Chapter 7

After the excitement, and to let Cassius rest, we sat on the road to catch our breath. I could tell that Anthony was eager to move forward, but by the look on Cassius's face, we really needed to wait. He probably needed stitches, but we didn't have those kinds of materials with us. We would have to reach civilization for that. I just hoped that Damian would be able to stop the bleeding.

After about ten minutes, which felt like a century, Damian took Cassius under the elbow and helped him to stand. "He's only going to get worse if we stay here. We need to find a healer, or even a farm—anything."

Everyone else rose and we began our walk down the road. I somehow ended up with Pumpkin, but I didn't mind. I was just worried about Cassius. I hoped the wound didn't get infected. We would have a much worse situation on our hands if it did.

I also still couldn't believe that Calum had gotten us out. She had somehow been able to see the door while the rest of us hadn't. It made no sense. Then again, neither did some kind of magical trap.

Although my mind was still overwhelmed with these thoughts about Calum and thoughts about everything that had just happened, what mattered most was getting Cassius somewhere we could help him.

But after the first bend in the road, everyone in front of me came to a stop. They just stopped and stared ahead, not saying a word.

I came to stand next to them to see, and what I saw was maybe the most confusing thing yet.

The road ended. And at the end of the road was a cottage. It was a rundown little cottage with vines twining through the windows and up to the roof. The roof and walls were sagging as if they were tired of holding themselves up. The panes were missing from the windows, and it looked like the walls had been patched with dirt.

The road wasn't supposed to end. The road was supposed to wind its way straight to the city Amartoth, the capital of the Central Kingdom. That wasn't right. Everything about it was wrong. The cottage looked eerie and forlorn, dark.

"What's this?" Anthony whispered in a hiss.

"Another trap?" Sebastian asked.

"Probably," Sterling answered, removing his sword from its sheath once more.

Damian let out a sigh. "Everyone ready?"

There were nods all around, everyone resigned. We had hoped too soon and celebrated too soon. It had all been too good to be true.

Sebastian tried to lighten the mood. "Who knows, maybe whoever lives here is nice."

All he got was a glare from Anthony.

Then, we were all moving forward, and as we neared the cottage, I realized how dilapidated it was. It looked like mold grew all over the outside. It was rotting, and it smelled like it, too. As we got closer, I could also smell a fire burning, and there was a wisp of smoke coming out of the chimney. Someone was home.

Damian held back, supporting Cassius as the others moved forward, swords drawn. Upon reaching the door, Sterling reached out his hand to open it, but before he could, it opened all on its own. Everyone took a step back as a very, very old lady hobbled outside.

She was the oldest woman I had ever seen. Her back was hunched. Her hair, which had almost completely fallen out, was covered up with a pointed hat. Her hands, pretty much only made of bone, grasped her cane for support. As she lifted her face to look at us, I couldn't help but stare at her frightfully long nose. There was even a wart on it, to top everything off.

Most frightening of all were her eyes. We all stiffened upon seeing them, for they were goat eyes. I knew they were goat eyes since they had rectangular pupils. The rest of the eye, or what should have been the whites of the eyes, were yellow, like a snake.

"Witch," Anthony seethed and stepped close enough to her that the tip of his sword was just an inch from her nose. His anger radiated off him in waves. It was so powerful I could feel it in my bones.

His assumption was due to her appearance and the fact that the trap probably belonged to her. A witch was a thing out of a fairytale book, but after being trapped in there with that monster, I couldn't think of another explanation for what this woman was.

The old woman just looked up at him and gave a quick cackle. "Well, of course, I am a witch, boy."

She tutted and turned to the rest of us.

"My goodness, you are quite a large group, aren't you!"

No one moved, but Sterling spoke, "What do you want?" His eyes were hard, and he looked unfazed by her eyes—and by what she had just admitted.

She hummed and scratched her chin, eyeing each one of us.

"Which one of you could see the door?" she finally asked.

A stillness came over the group, and no one moved. They were certainly a loyal bunch.

"What does it matter?" Damian replied, chin raised in defiance.

She cackled again. "I have been alive for many years, boy. No one has ever escaped my trap. But one with magic . . ." Her eyes roamed over us. "Yes, only one with the gift would be able to see my door."

We all stood silently, pondering her words. I knew none of us had magic unless Calum had some kind of power I didn't know of. But no, that was impossible. I had known her for many years and there was never any magic. It had to be some kind of trick.

Anthony spoke first, his sword still raised. "Listen, old hag. You're going to let us go right now. You're going to bring us to the real road, and you're going to do it now. Start walking."

He motioned with his sword for her to move. His anger permeated the air like a fog. All he wanted to do was go home, and he was done playing games. The look in his eyes was dangerous, and it made me very happy he was on our side.

She turned to look at him like he was a fly that needed to be swatted from her window. "Don't be ridiculous."

And with a flick of her finger, his sword was gone. It was gone—as if it had never been there. Anthony's hand closed around thin air, and his eyes widened in alarm.

"Now . . . let's see." Her eyes continued to roam over us like she was inspecting us.

Then they landed on Calum and paused, narrowing slightly. "My dear, you got these boys out of my trap, didn't you?"

I reached out my arm to put something between her and the witch, but Calum spoke softly and simply replied, "Yes."

The witch then smiled and nodded. "Yes, I can feel it. The magic."

"What magic? What do you mean?" Calum stepped forward, and I reached out to take her arm in warning.

I tried to reason with her. "I don't think she's telling the truth, Calum. I think this is another trap."

There was no way Calum had magic. The witch had to be lying.

"It's definitely a trap," Anthony agreed, but the others just looked between her and the witch, unsure what to believe and what to do.

"This is no trap." The witch was starting to look annoyed. "I'll prove it to you."

Her eyes landed on Cassius, who was looking paler and was now starting to have cold sweats.

She smiled as if pleased with herself. "Ah, you ran into my pet."

Then, she waved her hand in his direction. At first, it appeared nothing had happened, then Cassius stood a little straighter and looked around as if he was seeing everything for the first time. His eyes were more alert, and then he stepped away from Damian's support and reached for his arm bandage. He pulled it away and there was nothing there, no gash, nothing. There was only some leftover blood on otherwise unharmed skin.

Everyone stared in shocked silence. The woman definitely had some unnatural abilities. If you had told me a few days ago that there was such a thing as witches, I would have never believed it. But after seeing a real monster, an invisible door, and what had just happened with Cassius, there was no denying that, perhaps, there was such a thing as magic.

The witch beckoned toward Calum. "Come, my child."

She stepped forward, but I stayed beside her, wary, same as the others. Even though she had just healed Cassius, that didn't mean she wouldn't try something else more sinister.

"Hold out your hand," the witch instructed.

Calum did as she was told, and the witch turned her hand over so that it was facing palm up. Then she cradled Calum's hand with her own.

Again, it seemed at first that nothing happened. I looked into Calum's eyes to see if she felt anything. Her eyes never left those of the witch, and as I looked into those eyes, I began to see a soft glow. At first, I thought maybe it was the reflection of the sun, but then they began to glow brighter. It wasn't a white light, but a subdued, darker hue, an earthier hue. As her eyes brightened, the color became clearer. It was the color of life, the green of nature. It was like sunlight through a canopy of leaves.

The others also saw, and they stared, like me, dumbstruck.

Then, my eyes were pulled away from hers by the glow of something else. The light was also held in the palm of her hand. It was a glowing orb the size of an egg. It sparkled, tendrils of glow wisping out to brush her fingertips. It was like a star, a living thing.

Then, the witch gently curled Calum's fingers up to douse the light, closing her hand, and it was gone.

"Ah," the old crone spoke into the silence. She patted Calum's closed fist. "The power of nature, very rare and beautiful."

"Power of nature?" Calum questioned, confused, her small voice sounding large in the quiet.

"Yes, and when I am done teaching you, you will be able to harness all magic."

Finally, Damian spoke up. "I'm sorry, but that can't happen."

I felt relief at his words. The witch could not be trusted. She was evil. She had made that trap. That creature was her pet. She had let the others waste away in an endless cycle of fear and loneliness. That wasn't right. There was something wrong with the whole picture.

"Calum . . ." I began to speak, but she interrupted, startling me.

"Wait!" she demanded, and she even seemed to startle herself with the abruptness.

"I . . . um . . . do I really have magic?" Calum asked softly, her eyes searching the witch's face, their hands still clenched together. There was something in her eyes I couldn't explain.

"Yes, my dear." The witch smiled, and I saw from the look on her face that she knew she had won.

"Then . . . I would like to learn." I could see longing in her eyes. She wanted to have magic. She wanted to have something that made her stronger, safer, something that was her own.

We all stood stunned until Damian spoke.

"Calum . . . let's talk in private for a minute."

I watched her hesitate. She didn't want us to change her mind, but she relented.

"Okay," she barely whispered.

I took Calum by the arm, and the witch released her hands, letting us lead her a safe distance away.

I was the first to speak, "Calum, there's something wrong about this whole thing. Remember that terrible creature in her trap? That's her pet. She let these guys stay trapped in there and look at her! Look at her eyes!" I looked deep into her eyes, trying to plead with her.

She took a deep breath, and let it out, looking around at all of us, one at a time.

"I know what she's done . . . and . . . I understand. But this is real. I can feel it inside me now. It's me. It's all me." I could see her struggling to find the words as she continued. "I want to do this. It's been inside me all this time, and I didn't even know it was there. It's hard to explain. But she said she can teach me, and I'd like to try."

Her eyes landed on mine, and it felt like she was staring into my very soul. She zoned in on our bond, our connection, to make me understand. "Please, Adric, just give me this."

And I couldn't say no. The way she looked at me, there was nothing else. She had never so blatantly asked for anything before, not like that, and it clicked in my mind why she wanted that so badly. She had told me, before we had entered these woods, that she had always felt like a burden, prohibiting me from having a life. Maybe that was her way of finding something—that one thing—that was hers. If she could take care of herself, then she wouldn't need to rely on me. She wouldn't feel like that burden anymore. Perhaps she could finally feel like her own person. She would be able to see herself as I saw her: beautiful, independent, monumental, a green island to my ocean.

"Alright," I whispered, and the others looked at me in shock.

Calum relaxed and smiled in gratitude. "Thank you, Adric."

Then, she turned and ran back to the witch who welcomed her inside her home.

We all watched her go in silence, and I knew they were also watching me, thinking Calum was my weakness. They certainly weren't wrong. She had never looked at me like that before, and there was no way I could have said no, even if it was for her own protection.

It was her choice, and she wanted it more than anything.

"We'll have to wait and see," Damian sighed and sheathed his sword, wording what the rest of us had been thinking.

Chapter 8

The day passed, and we found a river nearby. None of us wandered too far where we couldn't see the path, but we did look around. We took turns washing, cleaning, and sharpening weapons. We ate in relative silence as we waited.

None of us spoke of our concerns about whether Calum would ever come out or not. We simply assumed she would. We hoped she would, eventually.

And she did. As the sun began to sink behind the horizon, she came out to us. Her face was bright, and there was a smile on her lips.

She sat beside me where we were sitting in a loose circle in the grass beside the road. Her face was radiant with happiness, and it was so contagious I couldn't help smiling myself.

We all looked at her expectantly, waiting for her to speak, but instead, she reached out to the grass before her and closed her eyes.

I watched as a few blades began to wave in the breeze even though there was no breeze. They waved and then they began to grow, so slowly I watched as a small leaf formed and then another. Then, she opened her eyes and let her hand fall back to her side.

"Adric, I can't do much yet, but isn't it amazing?" she gushed and took my hand, squeezing it.

I nodded. "It is, Calum."

Then, she turned to everyone, gratitude in her eyes. "Thank you all. Thank you for your patience and for waiting for me. I know you want to get home. We'll leave soon, I promise."

They sat slightly stunned, but Sterling spoke, "A few more days is nothing in the grand scheme of things." The others nodded in agreement and even though I could tell that Anthony did, in fact, mind, he kept his mouth shut. It made me wonder if Sterling had anyone back home. He was such a mystery, a warrior, that it wouldn't surprise me if he was alone in the world.

Calum turned back to me, the excitement still on her face. "Did you know that there is magic all around us? There are other people, all over the world, with magic just like me."

I shook my head. "I've never seen a single person with magic before. Are you sure?"

She nodded. "The witch told me. She says they are rare so you don't meet that many. All the fairytales are true, too. There are all different kinds of monsters and magical creatures."

I questioned that, "Really? But we've never seen any."

"The witch told me most magical creatures have gone into hiding."

I didn't feel like I could trust what the witch was saying. We still didn't know what motivated her to help Calum, so it was hard to determine whether she was telling the truth or not. It was hard to believe that any of this was true, but now that we had seen that monster in the trap and had met the witch, it was hard to say that any of the things she was saying weren't true. I obviously had no idea what was true or not anymore.

Calum sighed. "I didn't even know there was magic inside of me until the witch showed me, but she's helping me find it."

"Well, I'm glad she's helping you." I took her hand and squeezed it.

I wanted her to understand that I was happy for her and she smiled at me in return.

The night soon arrived, and we all fell asleep easily.

The thrill of the morning and the worry of the day lulled us into deep dreams.

The next morning, Calum was off once more to the witch's cottage, and she disappeared inside. We spent our day as we had previously, basking in the sun, setting traps for small animals, and sharpening weapons.

THE THINGS OF NATURE

The weather was warm enough that we could keep our coats off, but some of the boys chose to keep them on. Their shirts were worn threadbare after such rough usage over the years.

I could tell they were all becoming restless. After living a life that was always on the go for so many years, they were unsure of what to do with themselves.

Cassius kept glancing at his arm and at the rip in his shirt. Even though there was nothing there, and he had cleaned up the mess as much as possible, it still irked him. He gave it a scratch every few minutes.

Anthony paced. He paced so much an indent began to appear in the grass and dirt. He was deep in thought.

I couldn't help my wandering mind, either. With nothing to do, there was no end to the thoughts bombarding my mind.

I wondered if Calum truly had magic. It looked to me to be the case and the most obvious explanation. I couldn't get the image out of my mind of her glowing green eyes. If there was some kind of magic locked deep down inside of her, then it had to have been very deep down. It was crazy the witch had been able to find it, and it was also strange she would be so willing to teach Calum. There had to be an ulterior motive. It definitely seemed too good to be true.

When Calum came out with the setting sun, she was beaming like the day before.

When we sat to eat dinner, a few rabbits finishing roasting on the fire, Sterling spoke, obviously trying to break the silence. "How's the training?"

The tension of everyone wanting to go home was palpable.

But Calum didn't seem to notice. She was lost in her own excitement and happiness.

"It's going well! I'm learning quickly. It's all about tapping into the reservoir inside me. It was there all along, and it makes sense. I was always good with animals and plants. It's a part of me. Soon she'll open me up to learning about other kinds of magic like fire, wind, or mind magic."

"You're being safe?" I asked, lifting a brow.

She rolled her eyes at me. "Of course!"

"Just remember how she held these guys in that trap of hers," I continued. "She's not a good person, Calum."

She grimaced slightly at my words but nodded. "She's done nothing to harm me so far, Adric. I am being careful. I promise."

I nodded, accepting her answer.

"Besides learning how to find my magic, she's also been telling me about magic in the world."

"In the world?" I questioned.

"Yeah! It's amazing to think that there are other people with magic out there!" She smiled, but then her face turned down and she sighed. "And I did ask her why we had never met anyone with magic before. She told me that many with magic are hunted. People fear them and don't understand them, so they are forced into hiding."

I thought about this for a moment. It did make sense. If they were forced into hiding, then we definitely wouldn't have met any of them. Thinking back to our own village, I realized it took very little for people to grow fear in their hearts. We hadn't even known about magic then, and they had still hunted us down. I just hoped that when we got out of this mess, we wouldn't have to keep hiding like we had in the village.

I took her hand. "Well, I'm sure once we reach Amartoth, things will not be like that. They have people visit from all over the world. I don't think it's something we should worry about."

She nodded. "You're right. I'm sure we'll be fine. Besides, no one will know us."

"Sorry to interrupt," Damian spoke, his voice firm. "But Calum, we'll give you two more days, then we really need to head home."

She contemplated his words for a few moments, hesitating, then she nodded, resigned. "I understand."

We fell asleep side by side that night. Calum was so close, her hand beside mine, almost touching, but she felt so far away. It was the first time ever that I wasn't sure what was going on with her. She was so happy. I couldn't really understand it. I guess she was coming into herself, discovering what was deep inside. I knew nothing about her power or what it entailed. I had no idea if it was dangerous or not. It concerned me that I didn't understand, but then again, I guess I had never understood her like I thought I had.

After only a few days, our lives had completely changed. I just hoped it was all for the better. I didn't know what to expect when it came to our future, but we would figure it out, one step at a time.

I was jolted awake by a horse's hoof almost stomping on my nose. Hands were on me, and they pulled me to my feet, even before my eyes had a chance to open. I struggled, but the hands were impossibly strong, holding my arms at my sides.

It took only a split second for my brain to wake, and then I was seeing men all around us on horseback. There were at least two dozen of them, and they were thundering around, making a cacophony of stomping hooves and yelling. They moved so quickly it was hard for my eyes to catch any one individual in the dying embers that were our fire.

I looked around. It was still impossibly dark out which made it hard to see, but I could just make out the forms of our companions being held in the same manner I was.

"Adric!" Calum yelled, and I saw her nearby.

"I'm right here," I called back. She was only a few yards away from me, and I could see the relief flood her eyes as she finally saw me, unharmed.

I turned at the sound of a loud grunt beside me and saw Sterling struggling against his captor. His muscles strained under his threadbare clothes, and his face turned red with the effort. It was no use. He tried to reach out with his sword, but a bare, ridiculously muscled arm reached in front of him and pulled the sword free, the metal glinting in the moonlight.

I had to blink to make sure I was seeing things correctly, but yes, the man holding Sterling was wearing nothing to cover his muscled chest. I could just make out a leather strap across his body that held a quiver of arrows on his back. The man's bow rested over one shoulder, but that was all.

His hair was jet black and long. The top was tied back, away from his face. The rest was free to hang down to about the center of his biceps.

Looking around, I could see that the others were all similar—they were topless, armed with a bow, and had long hair, though it varied in shades.

As one came to a halt in front of me, I realized the strangest thing yet. The top half of him was normal, but by the time my eyes reached the lower part of his stomach, he was covered in hair, and the human melded into . . . horse. From the waist down, the man was a full-blown horse.

I couldn't help but stare. My brain couldn't register what I was seeing. I had to admit these beings were the most terrifying I had ever seen.

The man-horse moved past me, not noticing my stare, and stopped in front of the group, facing the witch's cabin. We all turned to face the same direction. The windows were dark, but smoke continued to slither out of the chimney.

"She is in there," one of them spoke, and his voice was like thunder. It was lower than any normal man's, and it was filled with power. It made me shiver.

The one in front stepped forward. "Rudcasta," he called out to the dark cabin, his voice so loud and deep it rang in my eardrums.

The rest stood still, the air filled with silence.

A moment passed, and then another, and finally the cabin door creaked open and the witch stepped forward. Distaste formed on her face, and she remained mostly behind her door.

"What do you want?" Her voice was a hideous croak in comparison to that of these creatures.

"You have broken the agreement." His voice rang with strength.

Her eyes darted around, sizing everyone up.

"I have not," she retorted like a child.

His front hoof stomped with impatience, and I felt the earth vibrate under my feet. "You have humans here, against their will."

"Oh, no, no, no. They are my guests." She tried to smile in a friendly manner at us. It was the fakest smile I had ever seen. The glint in her eyes said enough to confirm what I had always known.

"We have been watching you, Rudcasta. You cannot lie to us. You know the terms of the agreement." He stepped forward and took his bow in his hands.

Then, there was actual fear in her eyes, and she stepped forward, ready to proclaim her innocence, but only a terrifyingly ugly screech left her lips as the arrow found its mark. Her wail died as she fell backward, and I looked away. It had all happened so quickly I hadn't actually seen the man-horse shoot. Calum shrieked in horror at the realization of what had just happened, and I wanted to reach out to her, but there was no way.

A second later, a retching, gagging sound like someone was choking came from near me, and everyone turned to watch as Cassius fell to his knees, the creature holding him letting him go.

"Cassius!" Damian yelled and tried to wriggle free, but he was held firmly in place.

Cassius, on his hands and knees, shuddered, his whole body convulsed, and something came out of his mouth, trailing the darkest goo from his lips. It fell to the ground with a splat, a dark ball of slime, reflecting the moonlight.

Cassian groaned then and sat up to clutch his arm in agony. Wet, red blood seeped through his sleeve in the same place where the beast had torn open his arm, and the witch had healed him. It only took about ten seconds for his sleeve to become soaked, and he turned a shade of sickly pale. He began to slump to the ground, passing out, but the creature previously holding him reached down and caught him, swinging Cassius onto his back like he was a bag of rice. By the time Cassius was in place, he was unconscious. Blood dripped from his fingertips where his arm fell down the horse's side.

With one mighty stomp, the same creature squashed whatever dark thing had come out of Cassius.

The one who had talked to the witch and appeared to be their leader stepped forward. "We must hurry. They must ride."

A hesitation passed through the group at that, then we were being let go.

The leader continued, "We apologize for holding you. We did not know if you would try to protect the witch or not. We did not know how far she had gotten into your minds."

"No harm done," Anthony answered.

Calum and Damian instinctively tried to head for Cassius, but they were stopped.

"If you want your friend to live, then you must ride." The leader eyed them both, glaring until they relented.

The others mounted while I clambered up much less gracefully. I had been around plenty of horses in my day, but I had never owned one, and I had barely ridden. Pumpkin was the only horse I had ridden recently and it showed. The others, being soldiers, made everything look easy.

The creature before Calum didn't let her struggle. He knelt, front legs then back, so he was on the ground and much easier to climb onto. She clambered on, her dress hiking up to her knees. Then he stood again with a few practiced jolted movements.

The leader stepped closer to us, eyeing us. "Grip with your legs," was all he said, and it made me realize there was nothing to hold on to. I splayed my hands on the horse's back in front of me and hoped I'd be able to hang on.

One of the creatures grabbed Pumpkin's reins and our supplies.

With one last look from me toward Calum, we were off.

It was even more difficult than I had anticipated with no saddle. I kept slowly slipping off his side, and he had to help me readjust.

We thundered through the trees, leaving the false road and cabin far behind. The trees themselves seemed to part for us as we sped through them, their hooves thundering, and leaves scattered. They weaved in and out from between the trees as if they were weaving an intricate tapestry, almost like a dance. These creatures were huge, graceful, and at ease in the forest.

I could see that some of them had tails that were braided in intricate braids while some let them hang. But they were all trimmed neatly and were well taken care of. The same thing went for their fur coats. They did not smell like horses. There was a cleanliness to them, but also a brutal beauty. It was hard to explain.

Dawn was slowly making the sky gray and in the growing light. I began to see them all, disappearing and reappearing through the trees like shadows instead of in and out of the darkness. Soon we slowed and I looked ahead to see what we were reaching. There was nothing out of the ordinary. When we came to a full stop, the leader reached out his hand. It came to rest on something I couldn't see as if there was a wall before us.

"Come." He motioned to a few others, and they stepped forward to do the same. Their hands all stopped and rested on the invisible barrier and slowly, very slowly, it began to ripple like water, outwards from where it was being touched on the surface. The ripples undulated from each of their hands and expanded outwards, farther and farther. Soon, the whole wall was moving and it was so long and tall I couldn't see any edge.

But, unlike water, these ripples were slower as if moving through molasses. They reflected the sun's morning rays in strange rainbow-like colors.

The three creatures pushed harder, and then the wall began to melt. It dripped and thumped to the forest floor, making the earth wet with rainbow shimmering goo.

The whole wall fell, little by little, until just a few drops were dripping down the creature's arms. They flicked away the final remnants, and the forest went back to looking as it had before.

The leader turned to us. "The cage in which you were held is no more." His eyes roamed over us and then turned back to the forest ahead.

The trap in which our new friends were held all those years was gone, just like that. Then another thought occurred to me. That shadowy monster had been held in the trap. There were no more barriers to protect us.

A soft growl came to us from somewhere off in the distance. I felt myself holding my breath as everyone stood still, listening. It came again a little bit closer, and I felt goosebumps form on my skin. I wasn't sure whether the horse-men were a match for the monster and fear rose again inside me.

THE THINGS OF NATURE

The leader silently pointed to several of his companions and then nodded toward the noise. The chosen few took their bows in hand and notched arrows without a sound, then they moved away through the trees, completely silent.

The rest of us continued on, not looking back. They didn't seem to be concerned in the least.

I felt myself relax slightly. At least, I wouldn't have to see the thing again. I hoped they killed it.

We moved forward much more silently. The heavy hoofbeats from before were just a soft rustling through dead leaves.

As we moved through the Dark Forest, we left behind the dead, flat earth that I had become accustomed to. We began to make our way over tougher terrain. There were more rocks, undergrowth, and different kinds of trees. I began to feel the warmth of the morning sun on my skin, and as we continued to move, I noticed green buds on the trees. It truly felt like spring was in the air.

Nature was more alive the farther we traveled from the witch's cabin. Birds sang in the trees and squirrels darted through the first blades of grass. A gentle breeze rustled the branches of trees, and I found myself swatting spring bugs away from my face.

That was what I was used to. That was how it was supposed to be. It was like all the life surrounding the witch had somehow withered or been hidden away.

It was like she was surrounded by an evil taint that even life itself was not willing to touch. I knew then, deep in my heart, that she had been evil after all. There had been something wrong about her, and I felt quite relieved, calmer, the farther we traveled from that wretched place. I didn't fully understand why she did what she did, but it had been wrong, I was sure of it.

We traveled across rolling hills at a speed that surprised me. We crossed streams and through swaths of evergreen trees. We passed through berry brambles, and soon I could hear the soft sound of water rushing in the distance. We neared a river, and we turned to head upstream. After about a half mile, we came to a waterfall, which fell about ten feet before crashing into the pond below.

The water came straight out of the rock as the cliff itself rose much higher overhead, creating an impossible climb. There was no way up. We were heading toward a dead end.

The horse-men continued to walk, and we headed straight for the waterfall. When we reached the falling water, we headed straight through it in a single file line.

When it was my turn to pass under it, I got completely drenched. The water was an ice-cold shock as it hit my skin. We humans shivered, soaking wet, as we continued through the dark tunnel. The horse-men didn't seem to mind getting wet in the least.

The tunnel was made out of black, jagged rock as if it were cut out of the mountain. It was a comfortable size, about eight feet tall by six feet wide. The hooves of the horse-men clipped loudly, the sound bouncing off the rock walls around us, creating a cacophony of noise. It was quite dark, but as we moved forward, the light behind us faded and a new light ahead of us began to grow.

THE THINGS OF NATURE

The cave opened up, and I sucked in my breath in awe.

Chapter 9

We looked down upon an expansive valley, and it was lush with life. There, it was summer, the air fresh and decadent with the smell of pine. Leaves were fully out on the trees, and the sun shone full and bright as only it can in the summer months.

What shocked me—what took my breath away—was the size of the trees. They were HUGE!

From where we stood, we were extremely high up. The valley dipped before us into a giant bowl. We could see over the upper canopy of these trees to the snowcapped mountains that wrapped around that magnificent place, protecting it.

The trees had to be at least ten stories tall. Their bases were between twenty and thirty feet across. It took me a minute to remember what that kind of tree was called, but then it came to me—these were sequoia trees. I had read about them and had been told about them by my parents when I was little. I had never seen one in person before. They were absolutely incredible.

The leader spoke, "You walk from here."

We slid off the backs of the horse-men. Only Cassius, still unconscious, a drop of blood falling from his fingertips every once in a while, remained in place. My heart clenched at his pale face.

Calum and I walked side by side down the mountain path. It was steep with crumbling rocks, and I ended up taking her hand to keep us both steady.

It took us a while to get to the bottom, but once we did, there were others to greet us. There were more horse-men, and I was surprised to see horse-women as well, even a few children, some of them my height. They greeted each other with smiles and clasped arms.

Where the men wore nothing but their weapons, the women covered themselves in pieces of animal hides. They used small strings of the hide to tie back their hair in intricate braids and bands wrapped around their upper arms and chests. They also adorned themselves with all kinds of flowers in their hair or tails or even their clothes. They were truly quite breathtaking.

My attention was pulled back to Cassius as one of the males picked him up like a baby, then handed him over to a female who had no trouble carrying the fully grown soldier.

Cassius's breaths were shallow, and he was still so pale, losing blood from his still-open wound. His head rested on the woman's shoulder, and the way she held him made him look like a young child, peacefully asleep.

She was different from the others. Her skin held black ink, which swirled around her eyes and cheeks. It came down her arms in different patterns and ended only at her fingertips. Her horsehair was all black and white splotches to match her skin.

"Come," she spoke, and her voice was also deep, regal. It made me think of an old queen, persisting on her throne.

We followed without hesitation, and I could feel the eyes of the men and women following us. They looked as fascinated with us as we were with them. They were friendly enough and willing to help, especially since they knew we had been in the clutches of that witch. They also probably understood that they had nothing to fear from us. We were weak, small creatures compared to them.

"Can you help him?" Damian asked the female, catching up to her. His eyes held deep concern, and I could almost feel the distress and worry hanging over us like a cloud.

"I do not know what else the witch cast inside of him. I make no promises," she answered, and after walking for a few silent minutes, weaving on a small, dirt path through the giant trees, we came to one with an opening.

The roots of that particular tree were parted enough that we could walk through them to the base of the trunk where an oval-shaped opening appeared, a doorway.

She stopped us, blocking the way. "You must let us care for him now."

She continued by herself, entering the arch of the tree, then was gone.

We stood there without direction, not knowing what to do besides look at each other.

That was surely Cassius's best option for survival. Whoever these people were, they had known the witch, and they knew how to deal with magic.

Calum took my hand and squeezed it. She was still there, and so was I. We were okay.

"Centaurs, huh?" Sebastian shook his head as if trying to shake a dream.

"Is that what they're called?" I asked.

The others all nodded. Apparently, Calum and I were the only ones who had never heard of them before.

"I just can't believe they actually exist," Damian said, staring after where the female centaur had disappeared.

"I just hope Cassius is okay," Calum said softly.

"Me too." I squeezed her hand in reassurance, giving her a soft smile.

We ended up sitting on the giant roots of the tree as we waited. There was nothing else to do.

Centaurs passed us by every so often. When they saw us, they gave us gentle nods and soft smiles as a greeting. They carried baskets filled with fruits and vegetables or rope from which rabbits and squirrels dangled.

From what I could tell, it was a full-blown town. They were hunters and gatherers of the forest, and it was interesting to watch them carrying on with their day. They worked and rested the same as normal people.

After some time passed, a young female with two of her friends, around our age, came up to us. Her hair was blonde, waving in perfect curls down her arms and back till it met her elbows. The curls were perfect and well cared for, but because they were so long, she still appeared a creature of the woods.

They carried a bowl in each of their hands, and they handed one to each of us. A fragrant soup wafted up to meet me, and it smelled delectable. Steam rose from the surface, still hot.

"It's rabbit," she explained, and her voice sounded like wind chimes, soft and resonant.

"Thank you," Damian responded.

We all smiled our thanks in turn.

"You must be hungry."

I could tell she was interested in us. Unlike her two companions, who were nervously looking at each other, she wanted to know more.

"It was a long journey," Sebastian commented, and I could see in his eyes that he wanted to keep talking to her as well.

It had been a long journey, at least for them. It had taken minutes to get free, but they had been lost for many years.

Sebastian's comment caught her attention, and her eyes widened. "What was the witch like?"

Her companions looked at her, hesitating, not as brave as she was. Then they left the way they had come.

"Evil," Anthony commented.

"I am sorry to hear that. We've allowed her to live here in these woods for a great many years. She's been around since way before I was born. But she broke the agreement. She harmed a living thing and trapped you all."

Damian nodded. "That she did and may I ask, did you all find out about this trap recently? Have you known for a while what she was doing?"

Her eyes widened again. "Oh no, no, no. She was very sneaky. We had no idea what she was doing until yesterday. You should have seen how angry the council was." She shuddered, reliving her memory.

I could tell that even though she was our age, she was quite innocent, probably coddled in that safe valley all her life. She certainly didn't notice how delicate the question was that Damian had asked, or what he truly implied.

Her answer seemed to satisfy Damian and he leaned forward, sipping at his soup. When he took his first sip, his eyebrows lifted quite a bit.

"This is delicious," he remarked.

She beamed at him. "I made it this morning."

Then she sat before us, her back legs under her and her front legs crossed in front. She was most certainly planning on enjoying our company for a while longer.

We all ate, and I did have to agree that the soup was particularly good. We didn't have any utensils, but it was easy enough to bring the bowl to our lips.

Calum was also quite pleased. I could tell she very much missed the comforts of home. But I knew the witch still troubled her. For that young centaur, it was obvious the witch had been evil, and they had tried to be lenient with her. I also knew from how she had treated the other guys in the trap that she was not a good person. Calum had spent a longer time with her and had become friendly with her. It would be harder for her to see the witch for who she truly was.

"Is there more?" I heard Sebastian say, and he handed her back his empty bowl, smiling widely.

She giggled at that. "Of course! But you must save your appetite for tonight. You must join us for this evening's feast, our honored guests!" Her eyes sparkled with merriment. She was obviously very excited about the idea.

"Feast?" Damian asked, curious.

"Why, yes! Tonight is our feast of spring! You arrived just in time!" She looked toward Sebastian, and I swore a slight blush tinted her cheeks.

"Well, we will definitely be there," Sebastian replied, smiling back.

Conversation continued and the sun became full in the sky overhead, then slowly passed to where it almost touched the great mountains surrounding us.

The female centaur then stood. "My name is Celeste, by the way." She smiled and motioned for us to follow her. "Your friend and our healer will not emerge for quite some time. I should get you all settled for the night."

We then followed her, twisting our way through the enormous trees. Many of them had openings like the one the healer had entered. They were evidently homes where these people lived, and I couldn't help but anticipate finally going inside one.

We had not traveled too far when Celeste entered into one of these trees and we followed.

The floor was the base of the tree, hard wood, and the walls rose up around us to about ten feet tall. A staircase made out of the tree wrapped its way around the edge of the room to the second floor. The steps were wide, perfect for a horse to traverse.

The main room had no fireplace, which made sense. It was strewn with soft ferns around the edges, and there was a high table laden with fruits and vegetables—the perfect height for a centaur. Small slats in the bark of the tree and trunk enabled light to enter. Herbs and other drying goods hung from the ceiling. It was very clever with the bits of light streaming in and the greenery on the floor and ceiling; it actually felt like we were still in the midst of the forest.

She continued upstairs, and we continued to follow. The second floor had mats of fern and grass over feathers and soft down. These had to be beds, but they were almost like nests.

She gestured toward them. "This is where you'll be staying. I know it can be easy to get lost, but anyone you ask can help you find your way."

We thanked her then, and she left us alone to take off our swords, packs, and coats. We each claimed one of the beds and placed Cassius's things on his.

"I just hope these centaurs know what they're doing," Anthony whispered.

Sterling clasped him on the shoulder. "They're his best hope."

When we headed back downstairs there was something else on the table in the middle of the room. There were new clothes for all of us, stacked in neat stacks.

I was grateful for that, and I could tell the others were even more so. They had been wearing the same clothes for quite a long time, and it was hard to keep such things clean. They were full of tears and holes.

There were also fresh pails of water on the floor, and I could tell the others were itching to get clean as they ushered Calum to wait outside.

Sebastian gave her a peck on the cheek, grinning. "We promise to save some clean water for you."

Calum rolled her eyes and sat herself on one of the giant roots.

It was a relief to finally become clean, but as the others washed up and put on their new clothes, it was like they were shucking off their old skin. They were becoming new, fresh, and clean, and they were leaving behind the darkness and the past few years crumpled up in a dirty pile on the floor. They all breathed fresh sighs of relief, and I could practically see the burden lifting off their shoulders.

They even decided to all use Cassius's razor to shave their faces, and when they were done, they all looked like completely different people. They looked younger, fresher, and fuller of life—not like soldiers exiting the battlefield. I could tell they even felt that way as they all grinned and were in high spirits.

When we opened the door for Calum to come back in, she was startled at our appearance. Her eyes roamed over everyone, and she smiled a big smile. "You all look fantastic!"

And I suppose we did. We all wore the breezy, cream-colored tunics and brown pants that clung to our legs, perfect for hunting and other sports in the woods. We had even all received a new pair of black laced boots.

I wondered where the centaurs had found these things, but I guessed it didn't matter. Perhaps it was magic.

We then left to give Calum some privacy, and when she finally came out, she wore a new dress.

The green of her dress, which was made out of giant leaves, made her eyes shine the same color. I had never seen leaves so big and they overlapped to make her skirt and cover her chest. Vines wound down around her arms from her shoulders and met at her wrists. The dress was form-fitting, except for where it left her hips and trailed off to where it ended at her ankles. She even had her own pair of laced, black boots.

"You look lovely," I commented, smiling.

She touched the fabric of her skirt and smiled in return. "It's a little different, but I like it."

"It's very you," I admitted, and it was. It reminded me of her shining green eyes and of the power she had held in her hands. It also reminded me of all those quiet days back at our cabin when we had been out in the woods together. When she had looked at me, her eyes were wide and full of joy against the backdrop of sunbeams and grand trees; she had always been happiest among the trees. The light behind her seemed to shine through her eyes. It made sense knowing she had the gift of nature magic.

    At that moment, Celeste returned, and there were new flowers in her hair and tail.

    It was time to go to the feast.

Chapter 10

We made our way through the trees once more, but that time, the sun had almost finished setting, and the twilight gave everything an odd glow.

We made our way toward the center of the valley where a warm light emanated. When we got closer, candles in cages sat upon the forest floor, and they became more numerous the closer we came as if they were directing us toward the center, lining our path.

When we reached our destination, I wasn't sure where to look first.

A giant bonfire sat at the center of the large clearing. Tall logs, creating a teepee, made the flames rise so that they were higher than me by several feet. Centaurs milled around everywhere, all decked out in fresh flowers. It created a sea of color across the glade. There were also blankets strewn about, and they were all laden with a variety of foods, perfectly fresh and fragrant.

"Come!" Celeste led us into the clearing to a large blanket with food layered at its center.

"Please sit! Eat as much as you like! I must go now, but please enjoy yourselves," she trotted off through the crowd and disappeared.

We all sat in a circle and began eating, hungry. The food was indeed fresh, dripping with sweet fruit and savory meats. We stuffed ourselves. It was just so hard to stop eating.

Calum groaned beside me, leaning back and putting a hand on her stomach. "I'm so full."

I laughed, and I had to agree.

The night finally encompassed us, and it was hard to see between the shadows of figures traipsing before the fire.

A boom sounded from the other side of the fire, drumming as a deep but light thunder. It came again and then again, repeating itself slowly as the centaurs began to clear a space around the fire, but two remained.

There was Celeste and another male centaur on opposite sides of the fire; they were circling, very slowly, to the beat of the drum. She was blonde and all light, whereas he was all dark, blending into the night. With each beat, they took a step, and she began to weave her arms in a chaotic and slow dance. The movements appeared random to me, but they probably were well-practiced. *Boom . . . Boom.* The steps became more complicated, and they began to dance to their own inner music, keeping time with the drum.

The beat was still slow, but the complexity of their steps increased, their legs and hooves weaving and twisting until they finally met each other. *Boom . . . Boom . . . Boom.* Then, they were stepping together, their hooves weaving in and out and they took each other's hands. The beats finally became faster, and they quickened until they were galloping around each other, and through each other, and I soon had no idea what I was seeing. *Boom . . . boom . . . boom . . .* then silence and stillness.

It was over, and they were still, facing the others. Hooves began to stomp the ground, creating a thunderous cacophony, and I realized it was applause. They bowed, and a soft sound, something like a lute, began to play a delicate melody and others joined in the dancing or went up to speak gratitude to Celeste and the male.

Calum startled me out of my stupor. "Adric! We should dance!"

She took my hand, and her eyes were wide and eager, looking into mine.

"Oh, Calum, no. We have no idea how to dance." I didn't want to look like a fool in front of these magnificent creatures. The music was something much easier to dance to, but there was still no way.

Sterling's voice rose over the music. "I'll dance with you, Calum."

I looked at him, startled again. He was sometimes so quiet I forgot he was even there, but he stood, wiping his hands on his pants. He offered his hand to Calum, who grinned widely and took it. He pulled her to her feet easily and led her closer to the fire.

I watched as he instructed her on where to put her hands, one in his and one on his shoulder. He placed his other hand on her waist and then he began to step, and she immediately looked down to their feet to follow his movements. They stepped slowly, moving one foot at a time, and I could see him speaking to her, instructing her where to move her feet.

I watched them as they danced together. Sterling was at least a foot taller than she was, for the top of her head only came up to his shoulder. She looked so small compared to him and his warrior muscles. But even though they were so different, they actually looked good together.

Calum smiled and laughed as she messed up her steps, and Sterling smiled in return, urging her to keep going. His hair shone silver with the light of the fire behind him, and it made me wonder if that was why he had the name he did.

As I watched, I found I couldn't look away, and as she gave him one of her soft smiles usually only reserved for me, I began to feel a jealousy, deep in my chest. I had never felt that kind of loathing before, and it was directed at Sterling—who had done nothing wrong. He had merely stepped up when I had not.

That was my chance. I would probably never get another opportunity like that. Even though we were in that new place, far away from home, our future completely unknown, there was no time like the present. There was no better way to light a spark than on an evening filled with romantic music and firelight.

I took a deep breath, trying to steady myself, and stood.

Sebastian grinned mischievously at me and gave me a thumbs-up. "You got this."

I laughed at that and felt my nerves ease with the humor. I told myself I could do it, and made my way through the clearing, dodging couples, and when I reached them, I didn't hesitate. I tapped Sterling's shoulder. "Is it alright if I cut in?" I asked.

He nodded, gave me a knowing smile, then stepped back. I took his place and my heart fluttered as I placed my hand on her waist.

Calum smiled up at me. "I thought you didn't know how to dance."

"You looked like you were having fun." I smiled and took a step closer so we were almost touching. It was the most intimate I had ever been with her, especially as I stared deeply into her eyes. We had been plenty close before, but the atmosphere was different with my hand on her waist and her hand in mine.

There was a moment of silence, and I had to clear my throat. "Sadly, I still don't know how to dance."

I grinned at her, and she threw her head back in a laugh; the mood immediately relaxed.

"I'll show you." She smiled and then began to teach me the steps Sterling had shown her. We both stared at our feet and laughed at ourselves and our sorry excuse for dancing. And since I was still feeling spontaneous, I twirled her and she squealed in surprise. She fell back into me, her eyes bright.

She was radiant in the light of the fire. The soft, golden glow lit her face and made her curls shimmer. The way she smiled made her whole face light up. Then her smile faltered a little. She had caught me staring.

"Sorry." I shook my head, embarrassed.

"It's okay," she answered softly, and a light blush tinted her cheeks. She looked away, also embarrassed by the moment, and then she laughed, grabbing my arm. "Adric, look!"

I turned and there was Sebastian. He was in front of Celeste, and he was bowing deeply. Celeste looked like she had no idea what to do, but as Sebastian reached out his hand for hers, she gave it.

Calum looked back at me and grinned. We continued our dancing, and since we were both such sorry excuses, we gave up on the complicated steps and reverted to just stepping back and forth to the music.

Calum spoke softly, appearing thoughtful. "I wonder what's going to become of us." Her eyes appeared distant, and I guessed there was probably a great deal on her mind.

I wasn't sure how to respond, but I took in a deep breath and let it out. "Let's take it one day at a time."

I squeezed her hand gently, and she smiled back. "Sounds good to me."

As the night wore on, we continued our dance. Neither of us made a move to leave so we stayed.

Calum eventually gave a big yawn and we both laughed.

"Sorry," she murmured.

"It's been a long day," I replied. I couldn't believe that just that morning we had been carried away from the witch's cottage.

Then, before I realized what was happening, Calum laid her head on my shoulder, closing the distance between the two of us. I felt myself stiffen in surprise but relaxed and wrapped my arms around her. I could feel her soft breath on my neck and her wild hair tickled my chin. She had her arms wrapped around my middle, and her body pressed against mine.

We stayed like that, and I knew that at least we still had each other. That was never going to change, and even if she didn't feel anything romantic toward me, we would always have that closeness.

When the song finished, she pulled away. Her cheeks were flushed with warmth and her eyes heavy with sleep.

"I think it's time we get some sleep," I murmured, and she nodded.

She let me lead her back to where the others were sitting, her hand in mine.

"We're turning in," I announced, and the others looked up at us sleepily.

"We'll join you," Sterling answered, and they rose stiffly.

Celeste must have seen us because she came over beside Sebastian.

"I'll bring you back," she spoke and led the way through the woods.

As we wound ourselves through the trees, the light behind us dimmed. The candles dwindled and some of them were already out. I expected the darkness to surround us, but instead, there was a soft, silvery glow, and I realized it was emanating from the stars. They were so bright there as if they were closer to the earth.

When we reached our destination, Damian paused.

"Is there any news on our friend?" he asked Celeste.

She shook her head. "I'm afraid not. I'm sure there'll be an update in the morning."

She turned to leave, then turned back, remembering, "Oh, and I'll be here early to get you. I'll be taking you to see Her."

"Her?" Damian questioned.

She smiled softly, her eyes going distant. "You'll see. Get some sleep." Then she turned and trotted away.

The inside of the tree was completely dark, but we made our way upstairs and collapsed. The beds were ridiculously soft, and I fell asleep instantly.

Chapter 11

The smell of delicious food wafted up the stairs and woke us. Upon heading downstairs, we found food laden on the table and buckets on the floor for us to wash up with, like the previous day. There were also fresh clothes, and the dress Calum received was much more pedestrian, like the clothes the boys and I wore.

We were going to be seeing Her today, whoever that was. Perhaps she was their leader. Maybe she was the healer who had taken Cassius. We would soon find out.

Celeste came as she said she would and led us through the forest once more. That time we continued past the central clearing and toward the far side of the valley. When we reached the base of the mountains, we began our upward ascent. The path was again plenty wide enough for a horse, but it was still slippery with loose rocks.

We didn't end up climbing too far. We just reached the point where we entered into the tree canopy, and then the path leveled out and widened. There was a grassy plateau about ten yards by ten yards, and it was covered in ferns, short grasses, and soft mosses.

There were already three other centaurs there and they stood off to the side, facing a cave entrance in the cliffside. There was also a human, sitting and facing away from us, and we recognized him immediately.

"Cassius!" Calum called and ran toward him. He smiled and stood. He looked perfectly healthy except for the sling around his neck, holding his arm.

Calum threw her arms around him, and he hugged her with his good arm. The rest of us joined in and covered him in a flurry of questions.

"Are you okay?"

"How are you feeling?"

"How bad's the arm?"

He laughed and released Calum. "I'm doing well, thank you. I've actually been waiting here for you all. I've been told that She will explain everything."

Then there was more embracing, clapping on the back, and smiles. The mood lightened immensely. The relief was palpable, and it was only when Celeste stepped forward and told us to sit that we finally calmed down and sat on the soft moss.

The glade fell silent as we faced the cave entrance. A fawn then emerged. She was the size of a newborn, her hooves the width of a nickel. Her eyes were large, soft, and brown. Then I realized she had no spots. Her coat was that of an adult doe, and I found myself confused.

This had to be the *Her* Celeste had mentioned. Perhaps she was something like a leader to them. But then she spoke, and for some reason, it all made sense.

"Cassius, Adric, Calum, Damian, Sebastian, Sterling, Anthony." Her eyes landed on each of us as she spoke each of our names. It made me feel like she was staring into my very soul the way her eyes looked deep into mine.

By that act alone, I could feel through her matronly voice that there was some kind of ancient power at work there. Whoever or whatever she was, she was tiny, delicate, but old—extremely old beyond her physical form. It was a strange combination. In fact, it really felt like a motherly or peaceful sort of presence. She gave off the feeling that we were being taken care of, watched over.

"There is a great deal to discuss with you all. I'm sure you have many questions," she continued and sat before us on a raised mound of moss, her legs folded beneath her like a cat.

Her eyes slid over us once more, and I felt that ancient aura around her.

"Your friend here suffered a grave injury at the hands of Rudcasta. You see, she used a form of magic that she should not have been able to possess. Therefore, it was twisted and wrong. But do not worry. He should be fully healed in a day or so with much rest."

There was a moment of silence while we took the information in. Cassius was going to be just fine and that was certainly a relief.

Calum then spoke up beside me, surprising me. "What do you mean twisted and wrong?"

The doe turned her attention to Calum.

"I understand your concern. You yourself have a great power, Calum. In fact, it is greater than you realize. A great deal of responsibility comes with such things, but do not worry, Rudcasta did not have time to corrupt it or you. It was most important that we stopped her teachings as soon as possible. If she had gotten her way then she would have simply used you for your magic."

"Well . . . I guess I'm having a hard time understanding why she was so evil. She was so nice to me, and she helped me." Calum looked truly forlorn, and I knew that she always saw the best in people. For someone to choose to harm another living thing; it was just hard to comprehend.

The doe nodded. "It is what the witch desired, power above all else, and she never had enough. Now, she was born with the gift of mirror magic, just like you were born with the gift of nature, Calum. That was never enough for her, and she learned how to use many other kinds of magic, like fire, wind, healing, and light. She was never meant to have these. It is against the balance and against the laws of nature to have more than one gift. So, when she gained these new gifts, they were not pure or balanced. The only version she could achieve was a twisted and dark form of these gifts. Being so twisted, they fed into the witch's desires and also transformed her into the ugly creature you saw. This only occurs for those with magic. If she had maintained her purity and fed the one gift that was truly her own, she would have achieved a beauty inside that would have expressed itself outwardly."

"What's mirror magic?" Sterling questioned, his face serious.

The doe turned to him and seemed to smile. Her lips did not move, but her eyes lightened.

She answered, "Mirror magic is rare. It deals purely in reflections. Those with the gift can travel between reflections in a form of fast travel. They can also hide inside any reflective surface. The surface can be anything as long as it is still, and they can physically fit through it, like a lake or even a puddle. They can also see through these surfaces to any other still surfaces. It is quite unique."

"Is that what our trap was made of? Some kind of mirror magic?" Sterling asked.

"She has been on this earth for many years and has learned quite a few tricks. The trap was a mix of water, mirror, and mind magic. The centaurs were only able to catch and contain her with my help. In order for us to let her live, after all the evil things she had already committed, she made the pact with us to never harm or ensnare another again. She failed at this."

There was a moment of silence as we all processed that, and Anthony spoke up. "We really appreciate everything you've done for us, but I know I would at least like to get home. When is the earliest you think Cassius will be ready?"

The doe turned her eyes to Anthony, and her soft eyes stared deeply into his. Her demeanor changed slightly, barely. She hesitated before she answered. "I would give it two days minimum." Her eyes didn't leave him after that.

"Couldn't we stay here?" Calum spoke softly, unsure of the reaction she would get.

It occurred to me that it would be amazing if the two of us, at least, could stay there. We would never want for anything again, and we would be happy.

The doe shook her head slowly. "I am afraid it cannot be allowed. If humans were allowed to stay, even good humans, we would begin to lose the old ways, and we would lose our closeness to nature. This place would become tarnished and I would disappear to a different, purer place. Are there any more questions?"

No one responded.

She continued, "In that case, I expect all of you to do as you are able around the village while you are here. Living off the forest is a difficult task, and we need as much help as we can get. And please, do not mention this place once you have left. Our home is sacred and must remain so."

She then stood and made her way back to her cave, not making a sound with her pebble-sized feet.

When she disappeared, we rose and made our way back down the mountain. We were all in a better mood with Cassius back, and if we left in a few days we would be back on our original route, heading toward the city of Amartoth.

We spent the rest of the day helping out around the village. We began with peeling vegetables and cutting ferns, but we were soon swept up by some of the centaurs who had rescued us. They were eager to put us to work and show us their ways.

They showed us their techniques when it came to making arrows to fill their quivers. They even let us try our hand at shooting, but we quickly realized it was impossible. We were nowhere near as strong as them, and their bows were a struggle even for Sterling, who was barely able to pull the string back.

We learned that the centaurs were the protectors of this forest. They had hidden themselves away from the rest of the world like so many other magical creatures had. They did this to keep themselves safe, just like the witch had said.

We also learned that since they thought of themselves as the protectors of this forest, they had felt obligated to take us in, since they felt that the witch had been their responsibility. They never had human visitors. We were the first. It was humbling, but we were also thankful.

These people were of an ancient race, and they were closer to nature than any beings I had ever known. That was why they were the most well-equipped to help Cassius. They knew more about the herbs and plants of the forest than we did. They held information that was long lost to humans. They weren't magic themselves, besides maybe Her, but they had great knowledge.

That night, we feasted as we had before, but there was no dancing or candles or ceremony. There was simply sitting, chatting, and eating across the clearing as if we were all in one big dining hall. I even recognized some of the food we had helped to prepare earlier in the day, including pastries filled with fruit, shaped into flowers.

As the light faded in the sky, the discussion turned to returning home. Even though the men were labeled deserters, they believed they could easily set things straight and head home. They had families and people who had no idea what had happened to them. It was sad to hear them talk about their loved ones. It had always been Calum and me, taking care of each other. It made me think about how things would have been different if my parents were still alive.

"Adric," Calum whispered beside me to get my attention.

"Yeah?" I asked.

"All of them have a home to return to in the city. I was just wondering what we might do when we get there. What are we supposed to do?" Her fingers were worrying a piece of grass, and her eyes looked up at me anxiously.

"Well, I suppose I will find a job. We can find a place to stay. We can make a new home," I answered her, placing my hand over hers to stop her worried movements.

She sighed. "I guess I just wish we had a home to return to. Don't get me wrong, I'm glad we are done with the village, but I miss having that one place I knew so well." She smiled carefully and I smiled in return.

"Once we get there, we can make ourselves a new home, I promise."

She took a moment to ponder, her eyes off in the distance, then she turned back to me with a mischievous grin.

"You know, I think I'd like a job, too."

"Yeah?" I laughed.

"Yeah. I'm sure someone will find my talents useful." She reached out her hand to where she had been picking the grass, and when she took it back, the grass was perfect again, grown back and untouched.

She then placed her hand on mine, surprising me. "I want to help. I want to be useful, and I want to do something for our new home. I want things to be different this time around."

She didn't want to feel the same as last time. She wanted a fresh start, a chance to feel useful and helpful, not a burden. I had always wanted her to be happy, so I would do whatever I could to support her wish.

"Of course, Calum. That sounds like a great idea." I leaned over and gave her a quick sideways hug, and she took her hand back looking away from me, and I thought a soft blush reddened her cheeks, but it was too dark to really tell.

"Anthony." Celeste's voice pulled my attention away as she whispered beside me. I had only been able to hear because Anthony was sitting on my other side, eating quietly.

He looked up at her in surprise, and she gestured for him to follow. "Can I borrow you for a second?"

"Sure," he rose and followed her into the trees.

I don't know what overcame me, but I had the urge to follow them. I couldn't think of any reason why Celeste would want to talk to Anthony, of all people. All he wanted was to go home, and he was the most silent of all of us, so there was no reason to pull him aside. They had never even spoken before. Concern rose inside of me.

Perhaps it was animal instinct, but I excused myself from the group and followed them into the trees.

I stayed as far back as I could without losing them, and I could hear them talking. I was far enough away that I couldn't tell what they were saying. Then we reached the base of the mountain, and I knew where we were. They were going to see Her.

They began the climb, and I followed, unable to turn away. When they reached the top, I found a spot among the ferns to hide by the edge of the path. Luckily, there was a large rock there as if it were set up just for me. I could easily look through the ferns to watch the proceedings from there.

There She was as if she had been waiting for them to arrive. Anthony took a seat before her, like we had in our previous meeting.

In the gloom of the evening, it was rather tough to see. There were only a few lanterns set by Her and those solemn lights made Anthony's face and front gleam in the darkness. It was like they were in their own little bubble of light, and everything else had already succumbed to the night.

Her motherly voice filled the clearing in the quiet. "You must wonder why I asked you to join me."

Anthony's eyes rested on hers, waiting for an answer.

"I saw something in you, something so strong, I couldn't ignore it." She leaned forward then.

"It's your heart," She almost whispered, then she touched her nose to his chest, right over his heart.

He didn't move, and she pulled back.

"There is something missing," She concluded.

And after a few seconds, Anthony responded. "I don't know what you mean."

His face was unreadable as if he had put up a wall inside of himself. He always looked like that, grumpy and unreadable. It was his defense against having any kind of emotion. He didn't want to look weak.

She just smiled sadly. "It's the other half of your heart, it's missing."

Then realization dawned in his eyes. "Beatrice." He breathed out her name like a prayer, his eyes widening.

I wasn't sure how he made the connection, but he did. Then his brow wrinkled slightly in confusion. "Wait, what do you mean missing? When we head home in a few days, I'll see her again. We will be together soon."

She hesitated, then sighed, and I immediately got a sinking feeling in my gut. Damian had mentioned earlier that she had been very sick, and I wondered if by missing, the doe meant missing from the earth altogether.

"I searched for her after you left this morning, and I found her." She hesitated once more, this time trying to find the right words.

She almost whispered the final word. "In the beyond."

I watched as Anthony's face crumbled. I had never seen him display so much raw emotion before.

"You mean dead?" he questioned, wanting to make sure he heard her correctly.

She merely nodded, and with that answer, he became suddenly angry.

"Damn it!" he burst out, grabbing his hair roughly with his hands, and a sob racked through his body.

"I should never have left. The whole mission was so dumb!" He hunched forward looking broken and covered his face with his hands. "It's all my fault," he concluded more quietly, and he looked completely drained. His outburst of anger was gone, and all that was left was a broken creature.

"It's not the end, Anthony," the doe tried to reassure him, but he turned his anger toward her, looking up from his hands, his eyes blazing.

"What do you mean it's not the end? She was everything to me. Everything! You could never understand." His eyes bore angrily into hers, but she remained calm, unmoved. She just continued to look sorry for him.

"If that is the way you feel, then there is something I can offer you," She pronounced gently.

"Like what? Bring her back?" He looked at her skeptically, and she shook her head.

"No, but I can bring you to her."

He eyed her, not trusting her. "What are you proposing?"

She took in a deep breath. "I see your bond. I see its strength, and I understand. It is rare for most to find that someone, the person that completes them. You did. And only because of this will I give you the choice."

Her voice was stern and commanding. "You can choose to stay here. Live out your life. She will be waiting for you. Or," She paused, "you can leave this place and join her in the beyond."

Anthony eyed her warily, pondering her words. "I'll die?"

"Yes," She answered simply.

"Fine," he had made up his mind, and his eyes flickered with determination. "I want to go."

"Are you sure?" the doe asked, wanting to make sure he had thought it through.

"I know where I belong and it's not here."

"Would you not wish to wait until the morning to see how you feel then?" She countered.

"I've waited long enough."

"So be it." The doe stood then, and the centaurs who had been watching the whole exchange stepped forward and moved the lanterns away. The doe also took several steps back, leaving Anthony alone at the center. The air was filled with silence, and I didn't dare move.

I had no idea what was about to happen and fear rose in me. I desperately hoped that Anthony wouldn't die. He still had the rest of his life ahead of him. It was hard to fathom that he wanted to die. But I had seen the determination and resignation on his face. He knew where he belonged.

It made me think of Calum and it made my chest ache. Would I do the same thing to be with her? Yes. There was no doubt in my mind. I couldn't imagine a world without her in it, just like Anthony couldn't imagine a world without his Beatrice. This only helped me to realize how deep my feelings were for Calum.

"Farewell, soldier," the doe said, closing her eyes. She continued to stand still, breathing in and out slowly. It looked like nothing was happening, then the sky grew lighter as if the sun were rising. But instead of at the horizon, it was directly over us. Soon the light was as bright as if it were noon. Anthony looked directly up into it, but for me, it was way too bright. It was like looking into the sun.

He stared into the sky, and I could tell he was focused, searching for something. Then his eyes landed on something and they widened, finding what they were searching for.

"Beatrice," he whispered, and he rose to his feet as if to meet her. Then, he was reaching out to her like a child to its mother. He strained, reaching to her in that light. I saw his tears reflected on his cheeks as wisps of light began to wrap around his outstretched fingers.

The light continued to brighten, and I had to look away. It became so bright I had to shield myself behind the rock and bury my face in my arms. It felt like an eternity passed, but in reality, it was just a few seconds. One moment, my eyes were watering from the brightness, the next second it vanished, blinked out like a candle blown out with the wind.

I slowly uncovered my eyes and peeked around the boulder. It took me a second for my eyes to adjust, and in that time, no one moved or made a sound.

Anthony was on the ground where he had fallen, crumpled like a doll, empty.

One of the centaurs stepped forward and gently rolled him over. "He's gone."

And he was. I could see his lifeless eyes from there, looking blankly up to the sky. He was still, so still.

At that moment I began backing away. It took me several steps before I was able to take my eyes off his, and even when I did, I still saw them clearly in my mind, etched in my memory.

I had no idea what to do. I felt myself panicking.

If I went back and told the boys what had happened, they would never believe me. All they would see was

Anthony's lifeless corpse, and there was no explaining that away. I felt we had come to trust the centaurs, but with no proof of what had occurred, I thought that trust would be broken.

My frantic thoughts turned to Calum. She would hear me, and she would believe me. Calum saw the good in everyone and believed everyone was good. I had never lied to her before, and I wouldn't start then. Maybe she would know what to do.

I hastened down the mountain and back toward the tree we had been staying in. A light emanated from the second floor, and I knew in my gut that it was her, and I wasn't wrong. She was there, sitting on my nest, the lantern at her feet.

When she saw me enter, she let out a sigh.

"I went looking for you when you didn't come back, but after coming here, I didn't know where to go."

She stood and hugged me, sensing that something was wrong. She looked searchingly into my eyes.

"What happened?"

"Anthony's dead," I rasped.

She sucked in her breath, eyes widening. "How?"

So, I told her. I sat her beside me and told her everything I had seen. After I finished speaking, we sat for a few moments in silence.

Then Calum surprised me when she said, "He made it home."

"Wait, what?" I questioned, baffled.

"You remember how badly he was trying to get home ever since we first met him? He's been trying to get home this entire time because he wanted to go home to her! Don't you remember how even seeing me for the first time upset him? Adric, knowing that she is the other half of his heart makes sense now. She was the only thing on his mind. She was the one he was trying so desperately to see again. She *is* his home."

My eyes widened in amazement. "Calum, of course!"

I felt myself smiling with relief. That was something our friends would understand, and it was a hundred percent true. Anthony had gone home, and he was where he belonged. It wasn't a lie; it was just as close to the truth as I was able to get.

"And Calum, we should tell the boys when they get in. I'll tell them that I saw him leave, which is true. I'll tell them that he went home. They deserve to know."

"You won't tell them that he's dead?" she questioned.

"I think doing that will only make things worse."

She pondered my words for a few seconds, her eyes looking off into the distance, then she turned back to me, serious.

"What happened to Anthony is sad, but I think he's much happier now. I think if we do tell them the truth, they will blame the centaurs for his death. I agree with you there. I don't want to tarnish his happiness or his leaving by turning on the centaurs. They were only doing him a favor, not harming him."

"Thank you." I took her hand and squeezed it.

CHAPTER 12

The boys came home soon after Calum and I finished our discussion. Naturally, the first thing they noticed was that Anthony wasn't there.

"Where's Anthony?" Damian inquired, coming to sit on his nest.

"He's gone," I replied simply.

"What do you mean?" Damian raised his voice and everyone else stilled, looking at me.

"He went home," I answered, the palms of my hands beginning to sweat.

I was telling them the truth, the best of the truth, and the only truth that mattered.

"He went home without us?" Sebastian questioned.

He didn't believe that was even a possibility. I could see it on his face. He didn't believe me at all.

"It's true. I saw him go, about an hour ago."

They tried to process that, and Cassius was the first to retort.

"He couldn't have waited one more day? Jeez, I would have left with him if he had asked."

The others still didn't seem to quite believe it, but Damian relented, understanding. "We all know how much he wanted to get back to Beatrice. I just didn't realize how strong that impulse was."

They let the subject drop as they hesitantly nodded, agreeing with Damian.

Everyone got settled, and we turned the lights out. But the darkness seemed thick and Damian broke the silence.

"Let's leave tomorrow."

"What?"

"Are you serious?" everyone remarked in surprise at his outburst.

I could almost hear Damian shrug. "Might as well. Cassius can ride Pumpkin. We should be fine. And besides, we've waited long enough."

Sebastian snorted. "Sounds good to me. This place is way too nice for guys like us anyway."

And that was that. We would be leaving in the morning.

⋆⇌◉⇌⋆

At dawn, we packed our things and informed Celeste of our intentions. She was disappointed but agreed that it was perfectly fine if that was what we wanted to do.

We were shown to the base of the mountains, the same place we had arrived. We were given directions on where to find the road, and we profusely thanked everyone before heading on our way.

Anthony was not mentioned, and I couldn't help but feel a little relieved.

We made our way through the black rock cave once more and shivered as the freezing water from the waterfall hit us. Then we were out in the forest and heading toward the road.

We remained silent for the majority of the journey, and there was only a small discussion when it came to reiterating directions on what path we were supposed to take.

Calum and I stayed in the back, letting the others navigate. Cassius also remained with us as he rode on Pumpkin.

It was a quiet journey, and I knew everyone was thinking about Anthony and how he had left. The guilt ate at me, but I told myself that I had done the best that I could, and because of that, we had parted with the centaurs on good terms.

The sun was sinking past the horizon when we found the road. But this time, there was no whooping or smiles.

"Well, here we are," Damian said matter-of-factly.

We stood there for several minutes, taking it all in.

"It's not the same," Sebastian replied, and I knew that he meant it wasn't the same without Anthony.

There was a shadow on everyone's heart.

Cassius nudged Pumpkin forward. "Let's get out of these woods."

Sebastian snorted in response.

We were off, but the night soon caught up to us, and we stopped for some rest. We spread out our blankets on the side of the road; we were not stepping back into those woods, even if the witch was gone. They still looked and felt eerie. It would take a long time before her presence dissipated.

The next morning, we set off again; by noon, we could see the edge of the wood. Again, the line was obvious. The trees on the far side were not as old, they were less dense, and they looked completely normal.

Upon crossing that line, Sebastian stopped. A few tears had spilled down his cheeks. He wiped his eyes. "Damn it."

Sterling patted him on the back. "It's a lot."

"It is. We're finally out." Sebastian inhaled steadily to calm himself. "I just didn't think we wouldn't all be together."

Damian nodded and his eyes looked a little glassy, too. "I know."

Cassius changed the subject. "There's a place near here we can stay. I discovered it when I was searching for you guys."

"Near here?" Damian questioned.

"It's a wanderer encampment. We should fit in pretty well now." He smirked.

A smile spread across Sebastian's face and he wiped the tears away. "Ahhhh. It'll be nice to see people again."

We continued in higher spirits and by late afternoon, Cassius turned us off the road and onto a hidden, but well-worn path. We walked in the grooves made by many wagons, and soon we could hear the sounds of activity—there were many voices, the squealing of children, and the clanging of pans. Then wagons emerged. They sat stationary beside campfire pits and clothes dried where they were hung up between trees on strings.

The wagons were all colors with intricately painted designs. They were strong, sturdy, wooden things, and they were what these people called home.

They wore clothing of all colors, just like their homes, and decorated themselves in intricate jewelry and other finery. They didn't try to fit into any other town or village. These people were completely free, and as I watched them work and play, I thought that maybe there were worse ways to live. It could be fun wandering and seeing the world.

I also recognized them; they went through my village several times a year, trying to sell silks or spices. Some even tried to sell fortune-telling, but I had never participated.

For the most part, they ignored us as we walked through, but many of them smiled in greeting or waved. Then, Cassius stopped in front of one in particular and dismounted. All the wagons were so different it was easy for him to spot the one he had been looking for.

A young woman with a baby on her hip emerged and her eyes widened in recognition when she saw Cassius, and she grinned.

"You found your friends!"

THE THINGS OF NATURE

I immediately realized her accent was similar to Sterling's. Her hair was also white like his against her sun-kissed skin. I wondered if they were from the same region in the south.

She embraced Cassius, and he smiled. "I did indeed."

He reached out for the baby with a grin on his face, but she swatted him away, appalled.

"No! No! You must clean yourself first. You people have no idea how to stay clean on the road!" She pointed toward a bucket filled with water beside her wagon, and he sighed, rolling his eyes as he went over to wash.

She turned to inspect the rest of us. "I am Matilda. We have plenty of food here, and you may stay the night. Now sit!" She motioned for us to sit around her fire, and we did.

She got the fire to blaze brightly, then brought out her large pot and began to cook. Once Cassius was done, he came back and took the baby, who erupted into giggles. He sat himself beside Calum, and she grinned, sticking out her finger for the baby to hold.

When Matilda left for some more ingredients from another family's wagon, Sebastian eyed Cassius.

"Is she . . . ? Is that . . . ?" He stumbled over his words, and Cassius laughed as he realized what Sebastian was trying to say.

"No, no, no. She's not mine. I happened to be in the right place at the right time. You see, little Penelope here got a little too curious near a deep river, and I happened to be there. We became friends after that."

"And I have no desire for scrawny young men," Matilda spoke behind us, with a ladle in her hand, making me jump in surprise.

Everyone laughed at that. I thought she really didn't look that much older than us.

We then ate dinner, and the sun began to descend. Just as the light began to dim, Matilda spoke to us.

"Come." She rose, and I took Calum's hand.

Calum gave me a soft smile as we walked deeper into the camp, and I returned it.

Soon, we arrived at a larger space where makeshift benches and seats made from logs were strewn. Many people were gathered there, their faces illuminated by the fire at their center. They were all waiting patiently.

We sat with them and soon a woman rose from the crowd. She was of middle age, and she wore extensive amounts of jewelry. Rings covered her fingers, and her neck was laden with necklaces.

She eyed the crowd, and once all were silent, she began to speak.

"Long ago, there was a great evil, not like today where the greatest evil is man. There was no one to fight the evil in those old days but a select few. They were our heroes. Tonight, I will not be telling the story of a hero. Tonight, I will be telling you something different. I am going to speak of the fall of the age of heroes."

She took a deep breath, her eyes scanning the crowd, then she continued. Her voice was captivating, and along with her hands and her piercing eyes, she told us her story.

"Many years ago, there was a king. This king only cared about one thing. All he wanted was to be a hero, to be remembered, to be written down in all the books for ages to come. He wanted that legacy, that immortality that only doing a great deed would bring. What better way to do this than to slay a dragon?

"At that point in time, dragons were scarce, almost extinct. They had been hunted down by many heroes in the past, and they were mostly gone. Lucky for him, many knew the home of the final dragon. That final dragon was all that remained.

"This did not deter the king. He set off on his journey with his great sword and steed.

"Soon, he arrived at the home of the dragon, and he called out to it, challenging it, but it did not emerge.

"So, he stepped down from his steed and entered the cave, and there he saw the dragon.

"Now, what the king saw was not what he had expected to see. There was the last dragon, old beyond years and graying. His wings were shriveled and his teeth were brittle. When he opened his eyes, they were graying with loss of sight.

"This was not the dragon the king had signed up for. He wanted endless glory, not a dragon taking its final breaths. To the king's surprise, the dragon spoke.

"'Have you come to slay me, King?'

"'That I have!' responded the king.

"'Even if I am old and gray?'

"'I will do what I must!' the king answered, and the dragon was puzzled by this.

"'Surely, I am no harm to anyone here. There is no need to kill me.'

"'You don't understand, dragon.' The king was getting angry, and he stepped forward with his sword.

"The dragon sighed, and even though his vision was failing, his inner sight could see the true meaning of this visit.

"'Ahhh, selfish king. You kill me for fame and to be remembered, but know this. I will also be remembered this day. For you see, I will achieve what you truly desire, immortality. If you slay me now, I will rise again, stronger and more powerful than ever before. If you cared about your kingdom, would you not leave me here to rot and pass in peace?'

"The king did not listen. He was blinded by greed, and so he slayed the beast, the final dragon.

"Upon doing so, the king's sword turned black. The dragon faded to nothing as its soul entered into the sword, and the king did not see.

"To this day, I tell you, the dragon soul remains, waiting to rise once more. The moment the sword is raised to strike an innocent, like it had been to strike the dragon, the dragon will be freed."

When she finished, she gave a bow to resounding applause. The sun had fully set, and the sky was black with night.

"Time for sleep." Matilda motioned for us to move and we rose, leaving behind the storyteller and her audience.

We lay around the warmth of the fire. The night had become chilly, and Matilda brought out extra blankets, which we were all thankful for.

Calum ended up beside me as usual and she sighed. "That was an incredible story! I read tons and tons of books back at the cabin, but this was completely different. It was like the story was more alive, you know?"

I smiled. "I was never one for reading, Calum."

She rolled her eyes. "Well, it's different."

She turned to face me, rolling on her side. "These people are different, too, the way they live and dress. It just makes me wonder what the big city will be like. It will be exciting to meet all kinds of people from all over the world. I bet they've seen places we have only dreamed of."

"Well, there's nothing saying we can't travel the world."

Her eyes widened. "I hadn't thought of that before."

"There's nothing stopping us. We can literally go anywhere."

I would follow her wherever she wanted to go, whether it was across the earth or just to the city. But I wasn't going to tell her that yet.

She pondered my words, then smiled. "You know, let's reach the city first."

I laughed and reached out to give her hand a squeeze. "That sounds like a good idea."

We fell asleep under a canopy of stars.

Chapter 13

I woke to the sound of stampeding hooves, and for a moment, I felt an intense déjà vu. Waking up further, I saw there were no centaurs, and the fire we slept around was still bright with living coals. It was still early on in the night.

"Adric!" Calum grabbed my hand and pulled me upright.

I scrambled to my feet and saw soldiers everywhere. I recognized them immediately for they wore the same clothes Cassius had worn when we had first met him, but these were clean, freshly pressed, and perfectly fitted. Their hair was uniformly short, and they all wore matching swords and the insignia of Amartoth on their sleeve.

A group of them had thundered through the camp on horses, heading to the far side of the clearing. They were the ones that had woken us. The rest were mostly on foot, and they were going from wagon to wagon, banging open doors and checking inside each. It was like they were looking for someone.

They hadn't reached us yet, thankfully. There was still time to think.

"What's going on?" I questioned, looking around.

"We don't know, but they're surrounding the camp," Damian responded, strapping his sword belt on.

The others were doing the same. They were all preparing, throwing on clothes and packs.

I heard a scream and watched as a soldier pulled a young woman out from her carriage by her hair. She had wild, curly hair like Calum's, and she flailed angrily, trying to grasp her attacker. Another soldier grabbed her, and they hauled her off and out of view.

We all watched in shock and I turned to the others. "Is there anything you can do?" I asked them desperately.

They shook their heads. Cassius answered. "If they knew who we were, we would be in way worse trouble. We are still on the list of deserters."

My heart sank at his answer, and a gruff voice shouted behind us,

"Hey!"

I turned back around to see two soldiers coming toward us. One of them had his sword drawn, and I backed up instinctively, grabbing Calum's hand.

They had reached us.

The one without the sword pointed at Calum. "She looks like the picture."

His eyes were dark and unyielding, like he had seen too much in his life.

The others stepped forward to stand beside us, out of the darkness, and with all of them next to us, the men stopped advancing. They eyed us, and I felt everyone sizing each other up. I was pretty sure we won as the one without the sword pointed at Calum. "She needs to come with us."

Sebastian let out a bark of laughter. "Why?"

"Orders from the General," he answered.

"Why an innocent, young girl?" Sebastian persisted, and I felt ridiculously relieved that I had all of these men by my side.

And I wondered the same thing. There was no way they were looking for Calum, but maybe they were looking for someone who looked like her or the other girl with curly hair. It made no sense to me. It was wild an entire army was sent to look for one person.

They didn't answer Sebastian's question, and Damian interjected, "We promise you, this is not the girl you're looking for."

Two more soldiers came running up to the two confronting us, and one of them held a piece of paper. He handed it to the one without a sword, and his eyes widened as he looked at it and then back up at Calum. He handed it back without a word, and he drew his sword. The others followed suit.

"I am sorry, but she needs to come with us," he spoke, and there was no room for argument.

At that, Sterling stepped forward, and he completely blocked our view with his broad back. His massive sword was strapped to his back, and he spoke, his voice deep and threatening, "That's not going to happen."

He then reached above his shoulder and pulled out his sword. The massive blade reflected the firelight, and from that angle, he looked like a god of war. I suddenly felt bad for these soldiers. I didn't think it was going to end well for them, but they stepped forward, completely determined and undeterred.

Then, Damian grabbed Calum and me and pushed us back toward Matilda's carriage and the woods.

"You both need to leave, now. They're just going to keep coming, and we can't stop them all, only slow them down."

I fought back. "We can't just leave you here."

His face hardened, and he nodded toward Calum. "Yes, you can. For Calum, you can."

At that, I felt my insides clench in fear for her. He knew how I felt about her. I was pretty sure they all did after how jealous I was of Sterling for dancing with her.

"You'll catch up to us," I said, taking Calum's hand in mine and backing up toward the trees.

He gave a sad smile in return, then turned around, and with the others, raised his sword.

I grabbed my pack, turned, and ran, pulling Calum along with me. The second we began to move, the jarring crash of steel reverberated in my ears.

Then, we were in the woods, and we were running. I was almost blind in the complete darkness of the night. I stumbled several times, and when I finally almost fell on my face, we stopped. Taking in deep breaths, I realized I had to think. We couldn't just run into the wilderness without direction. I tried to think of where we were in relation to the road and the camp and turned us in the same direction we had been traveling on the road. If we traveled parallel to the road, then perhaps we could avoid contact with the soldiers, and perhaps we could still meet up with the others if they managed to escape.

We began to walk, and that time I tried my best to cover our tracks. As a tracker myself, I knew what they would be looking for, and I did the best I could in the utter darkness.

"Adric?" Calum's small voice met my ears.

"Hmm?"

"Do you think they'll be okay?"

"I'm pretty sure Sterling will keep them safe," I answered, thinking back to his giant sword and dark eyes.

After a few moments of silence, she asked, "Will we find them again?"

"I hope so," I responded, then sighed. "If we all continue toward Amartoth, we should be able to meet up eventually."

"Okay."

We continued in silence for a few more hours and then came upon a clearing. It took me a moment to recognize what I was looking at, but then I realized it was barley. We had reached civilization.

"Hold on." I took her hand, and we slowly stepped into the moonlight.

As we made our way through the field, a farmer's cabin came into view. Everything was silent, the windows completely dark, and the smoke that rose from the chimney was just a wisp.

I led Calum in a wide circle around it.

The crickets were loud enough that they covered any noises we made, so I wasn't worried about making too much sound. The moon was so bright out in the open that I wasn't worried about being unable to see something if it approached, either.

We soon came upon another house, and another.

It was amazing how, after being so long away from civilization, the smells hit us. There was the smell of hay, cows, and horses. The smells of livestock and people were strong, and it made me think of the clean forest town of the centaurs. It was a different world. There you smelled fresh herbs, foods, and the smell of earth.

Soon we relented our difficult path through yards and fields and stepped onto the road. Everyone was asleep, and it felt futile and a waste of time to continue as we had.

Soon enough, Calum whispered to me, "I'm tired, Adric." She still held my hand and had been lagging behind.

"Just a little farther, then we'll stop. I think we should stay in the woods, as well. The soldiers might come looking through here."

Though, as we continued, the houses grew denser. We were coming to the center of town.

I started to slow, thinking I should find a spot sooner rather than later when a voice rose up out of nowhere.

"My, you two are up late."

I jumped in alarm as the voice of an old lady cut through the quiet night. Looking around, I saw a dark form under the cover of a porch roof at the nearest house.

"We're just going for a walk," I responded, then groaned inwardly at how dumb it sounded.

"Yes, yes, I remember my youth, gallivanting across the countryside. Please, come closer. I'm not sure I recognize you."

At her words, I hesitated. If we ran off, it would look even more suspicious. The best thing to do was appease her.

I walked forward, trying to keep Calum behind me as much as possible. When we reached the edge of the porch, I stopped.

"Sorry to bother you," I started, but she shook her head. "I don't sleep much anymore these days."

She looked at us more closely then. We probably looked odd in our wrinkled clothes and with my pack over my back.

"Runaways?" she questioned, eyeing us up and down.

"Yes," I responded, hoping that would end the discussion.

"Well then, you must come inside and rest. I have plenty of beds, and I make a mean breakfast."

I was about to say no, then Calum squeezed my hand. "I think we should stay," she whispered.

She sounded exhausted, and, of course, she knew how to pull on my heartstrings.

THE THINGS OF NATURE

I sighed and turned back to the woman. "Thank you, so much. That would be very nice of you."

She clucked. "Good, good." Then, she showed us inside.

The downstairs was a small kitchen and living space. Upstairs there were four small bedrooms. She put Calum and I each in one, then headed back down the stairs.

The moment I heard her close the front door behind her, I crept to Calum's room. I wanted to make sure she was okay. But when I peeked into her room, opening the door a crack, I heard her soft breathing. She was already asleep.

I sighed and headed back to my own room.

I was concerned because we had not yet discussed what had happened back at the wanderers' camp. Those had been soldiers from Amartoth, and they had been looking for someone who looked like her. I knew they weren't looking for Calum, though. The only place where Calum had been seen had been back at our village, even then, the villagers had never really laid eyes on her.

I was also concerned that Amartoth was exactly where we were headed. I had heard how big the city was, and it would be easy for us to get swallowed up in the magnitude of people. I just hoped they found whoever they were looking for so they would leave us alone. It didn't help that there was supposedly more danger for Calum since she had magic. We would just have to be careful.

I would never let Calum be taken. That was one thing I was sure of.

It made me wonder. If she could practice and learn to use her powers, then perhaps she could learn how to defend herself. That would be a sight to see. I still barely knew what she could do. Perhaps that might be something worth bringing up.

I kicked off my shoes and pulled the blankets up. We had a lot to talk about the next day.

Chapter 14

The morning came and went, completely ignored, as we slept through it. I only rose when Calum came in and shook my shoulder, proclaiming that food was hot and ready on the table.

I followed her down to the kitchen where steaming hot bacon and eggs sat in great heaps on our plates.

"Thank you. You didn't have to do all of this," I said, amazed at the old woman's generosity.

She tutted and sat with us to eat. "You have a long journey ahead of you, and besides, my chickens lay way too many eggs for just one person."

We ate and made small talk, but mostly I watched Calum. She seemed a little sadder than normal, quieter. She was probably thinking about the guys we had left behind.

I knew we would both want to find them again if it was still possible. We had built up a kind of trust and camaraderie even after the short amount of time we were in those woods together. We had become a unit. We had each other's backs, and it was strange not to have them there with us. In a way, I almost felt lost or like something was missing. I felt directionless.

We finished breakfast and grabbed our things. We thanked her profusely, but she smiled and said, "It's not trouble."

She was sad to see us go, and I realized that she was lonely. Probably not many people came around for visits anymore, and I thought that if we ever went back through there, we should stop in again.

As the door closed behind us, Calum paused, thinking.

"What?" I questioned.

She ignored my question and reached down to the flowerpots, one on each side of the steps leading up to the porch. As her hand passed over each, they faded to a more luscious green and the wilted leaves stiffened. New buds formed on each, almost ready to bloom.

"It didn't feel right leaving without giving her something in return," Calum whispered.

She then took my hand, and I was surprised at her initiative as we headed out into the street.

There were people at work. Farmers with their tools or animals and wives with their baskets. Most either ignored us or gave us a curt nod.

It felt good to be with her out in the open. There was no more hiding. She had hidden back at the cabin due to her being so young, an orphan. No one would have allowed an older boy to take care of a young girl like that. But I had been worried that whomever she had been running away from would find her again. She had run into those woods, alone, for a reason, and I knew I could take care of both of us with my fur trading. The arrangement had made sense back then. But being out in the open was a breath of fresh air.

Although, as we moved forward and more people saw us, I began to worry. It only took one person to give us away. The guards could be notified at any time. But no one gave us a second glance. Either way, it still sat in my mind.

I finally voiced my concerns to Calum. "Maybe we shouldn't head to Amartoth," I conceded.

"What?" Calum stopped walking, jerking back on my hand. "We have to!" she exclaimed.

"Remember those guards last night, Calum? I know you're not the one they're looking for, but if they find us again, I can't protect you like the others could."

She sighed, but I could see she was resigned. "Going toward Amartoth is the only way we can possibly find them again. I'd feel terrible if they never found out if we got away or not. And what if one of them is hurt and they need our help? I can't just walk away from them, Adric. They did so much for us. Please understand. And I'm sure if the guards do find us, we can prove to them I'm not the person they're looking for."

I nodded. There was no arguing with that. I agreed it was the right thing to do. "I still think we should be careful, though," I answered.

She squeezed my hand. "Of course."

We continued onward and instead of the village dwindling and ending, there were even more people. I thought we had passed through the center of the village, but I had been very wrong.

The houses continued to grow closer together, and wagons passed us by with goods. By late afternoon, we passed at least one person every two minutes.

By the time evening rolled around, we had made it to the center of the town. There were taverns and stalls selling goods. We also passed by the biggest church either of us had ever seen. It reminded me of the towering trees where the centaurs lived, and we stopped for a few minutes to marvel at it.

In my bag, I still had my satchel of cash from when we had first run from the village. The clothes and food had all changed, but at least I still had something left. I was actually surprised to see that it hadn't fallen out on our journey.

As we neared a tavern for the evening, one of the stalls caught my eye. That particular one was selling silk scarves, and I pulled Calum toward it.

"Pick one." I smiled at her and her eyes widened.

"I don't need a scarf, Adric."

"Think of it as a safety precaution, to cover your hair."

She looked at me in surprise as she realized what I was getting at. The guards had mostly been after her wild curls, and although that wasn't a perfect solution, it made me feel better all the same.

"The green one." She pointed, and I smiled.

Of course, she wanted the green one. It matched her magic, and it always looked good on her.

"How much?" I asked.

"Two gold."

I laughed. There was no way. At least I was in my element there. Bartering to sell my furs, I had used similar techniques.

"Two silver," I replied, and he nodded, holding out his hand.

That was a more than fair price.

We then headed into the tavern and ate a light meal of stew and bread. I bought us a room for the night and was happy to see that I still had plenty of cash to get us to the city and then some. Then we would have to find jobs as soon as possible, and there was no way of knowing how successful we would be.

Our room for the night was also a surprise to us. The bed was so big it mostly filled the room. There was plenty of room for us both to sleep comfortably.

It was not weird for us either. Sleeping beside each other had become a normal routine. I knew the caveats of sleeping in the same bed, but neither of us cared. No one knew us there, and to me, it just made me feel close to her. It was comforting in that strange place, knowing she was safe and beside me.

We fell asleep and, in the morning, we were off again.

The day was clear, and we made good time.

Calum wore her hair covered, and she had it tied around the back of her neck. She looked like a farmer's daughter, out for a stroll.

As we continued, there were more and more wagons piled with goods, coming in from side roads and from behind. We found ourselves among the merchants all headed toward the city.

An older man pulled up beside us, his wagon full of pots and pans. "Need a ride?"

"A ride would be nice," I answered.

"Don't like seeing young ladies walking so far. You can sit on the end." He pointed to the back of his wagon.

"Thank you." Calum smiled and nodded at him.

We took our seats, and he started back up again with a jolt. It felt amazing to finally sit after walking for so long, and Calum and I took our time looking at the scenery and chatting about what the city might look like.

We were steadily climbing slowly uphill, and as we rounded a bend in the road, we were suddenly able to see. The side of the hill fell away and before us was the city.

"There she is!" the merchant called out to us, and I couldn't help but be blown away by its beauty.

The city sat on the far side of a great plain against the side of a mountain. It looked like we would have to cross several miles before reaching the city gates. The walls of the city gleamed white, as did the castle at its center. Roads wove their way to the city from every direction, and it made sense why it was always called the Central Kingdom. Everything came to meet at that one place.

Flags hung from every parapet, sparks of bright blue against the white backdrop. I imagined the insignia of Amartoth was on each one.

It was bigger than I had imagined, and I had never seen anything made by man that was so magnificent. The city cut into the mountain itself.

"It's beautiful," Calum murmured, and I couldn't help but feel a wash of excitement.

I grinned. "You ready?"

Her eyes gleamed as they met mine. "Definitely."

Our cart turned downhill, and we headed into the plain and through the tall grass. I realized that it was not grass at all. It was hay, wheat, and other grains in an endless field. That must be one of the ways they fed the city. It had probably been forested before, like the surrounding hills, but it was all agriculture at that point.

"Adric?"

"Yeah?" I turned to her to see concern had washed over her.

"I don't know how we are going to find them with all these people."

I looked back at the city and imagined there were probably ten thousand people there. It wasn't going to be ideal, but I was sure by asking around we would probably be able to find their families, and then we'd be able to find them. That was only if they had made it, of course.

"It just might take some patience," I replied, and she nodded.

By midday, we made it to the gates, and carts and wagons flowed in and out unprohibited.

"Keep your head down," I whispered, and we passed through the gates undetected.

There had been guards there, dressed in the clothes I recognized well, but their eyes glanced over us as they looked across the crowd.

The streets were made of cobblestones and they jostled us violently, making my teeth rattle. The houses were all side by side, several stories tall, and they were all well off. There were no slums or downtrodden parts of the city that I could see, which I found curious. There were flower boxes in most of the windows, some containing flowers, others herbs or vegetables.

Soon, we entered the part of the city that was the market. There were stalls all crammed in side by side. We were in a giant courtyard, and the noise was almost deafening with all the yelling for customers.

The wagon came to a halt, and the old man turned in his seat. "This is where I leave you."

We hopped down, and I shook his hand. "We really appreciate it."

"Any time."

Then he was off again, his wagon disappearing into the crowd.

It took us a few moments to get our bearings as people plodded on past us. After asking several merchants, we were given directions toward a nearby street filled with inns and taverns.

As we walked down the street, Calum surprised me by pulling on my hand, stopping me in my tracks.

"You okay?" I asked. But turning to look at her, I saw her eyes were dazzling.

"Let's go see the castle! There's plenty of time left before tonight."

I raised my eyebrows. "Are you sure? You aren't tired from all the walking?"

"Well, yes, a little, but we're finally here! Come on!" She tugged my hand in excitement.

"Okay, okay." I laughed and let her pull me up the cobblestone streets.

It loomed up before us, wrapped in its own gleaming wall. There was more greenery. Vines with flowers wrapped themselves up the sides, and small trees were planted every few yards to surround and remove the castle even more from the general public. I had to crane my neck to look all the way up to the highest peak.

"It's incredible. Imagine seeing this every day," Calum murmured, but after a second, she pointed to some glass structures near the castle's walls. "What're those?"

"I think those are greenhouses." I tried to answer her question, but I had never seen a greenhouse in person before.

"Can we take a closer look?"

I shrugged. "I don't see why not." And then I was being pulled toward the glass structures.

As we neared, I saw that they truly were beautiful. The glass reflected the sun, making the small buildings shine. A few windows were open a crack, and we looked inside to see an abundance of plants. Some were vegetables, some flowers and exotic plants. I had no idea what they were.

I watched as she reached out and touched one of the vines finding its way out the window. It blossomed in her hands.

"This would be a good job for you," I remarked.

She turned to me with an expression of disbelief. "This is a job?"

I nodded. "Someone has to take care of all these plants."

Her eyes widened.

"I would love this job," she sighed.

I could hear the desire in her voice as she turned back to the plants in front of her.

"Well, why don't we come back and ask tomorrow?"

A smile bloomed across her face in hope. "Really?"

"Of course."

Then she hugged me, squeezing me fiercely. I hugged her back, grinning.

Chapter 15

We found ourselves a nice tavern where we could eat dinner. It was crowded and smelled like bodies, but the food was good. The room itself was just large enough to fit maybe forty people. It was cozy with the soft glow of candles and the few lanterns on the bar.

We ate chicken and potatoes, which made my stomach quite happy. Halfway through our meal, a fiddler began to play in the corner, and we sat, enraptured by the music.

Even after finishing, we stayed as people clapped and nodded along. Calum and I even pulled our chairs closer together so we could sit side by side.

By the warm light of the candles, I watched her smile and clap along to the music; it warmed my heart. Ever since we had entered the city, she had begun to smile more. It was like she was more alive. She was out of a cage of gloom and awake.

I imagined she was picturing our future here as I was. I could picture us walking by the castle every day. We would come to eat here on the weekends. We would be happy.

It still stumped me as to why she was so unhappy before. Maybe she had been lonely. She had told me she felt useless and a burden. But she had things to look forward to, things to strive for. Even though the road so far had been tough, I felt the journey was worth it at that moment. Hopefully, things would continue to change for the better.

The door of the tavern opened, letting in some fresh air, and I looked over instinctively to see who had come. When I saw who it was, my body stiffened in recognition.

Soldiers were coming in, and at first, I thought they were there to enjoy the evening, but then I saw their eyes. They were darting from face to face, searching the crowd.

I turned forward in my seat and took Calum's hand in mine, squeezing it firmly, my heart beginning to race. I then leaned over to whisper in her ear, "A few soldiers came in. Just ignore them."

Her eyes darted to mine in concern, but she didn't turn to look. She wore her scarf, and we looked like everyone else. I tried my best to relax my body and not look suspicious.

With a quick glance behind me, I saw the two of them talking to the owner of the bar. They were asking him questions, but we were too far away to discern anything. The music and voices were too loud.

I could feel my heart racing. All I wanted to do was make a dash for it with Calum, but I knew that would give us away. The only thing we could do was sit.

As I was fixated on any movement the guards made, I saw them out of the corner of my eye heading back to the door. I hoped they were leaving. They must be. It was a false alarm. I needed to calm down. I tried to take in a shaky breath.

When I glanced over again, there were more soldiers than before. They were entering the building in a single stream. There were five of them, six, seven. The original two were merely opening the door for the others. A few of them had a piece of paper in their hands like the soldiers had at the wanderers' camp.

My hands immediately began to sweat. That wasn't good.

"Calum," I hissed, trying to grab her attention.

"I saw." She spoke just loudly enough over the noise that only I could hear her.

There was fear in her eyes as they darted from mine back to the fiddler and back again. She was looking at me, expecting me to know what to do. I had no idea. I was as lost as she was.

The only thing I knew was that if they were coming for her, I was going to put up a fight. I still had my old sword hanging by my side, and I wasn't afraid to use it, not anymore. I'd do anything for Calum. My instincts told me to protect her at all costs.

The first few soldiers made their way behind us, and they blocked the stairs to the upper floors. By then there were at least ten of them, and they had drawn the attention of everyone in the crowd. The fiddler was the only one undistracted.

I let myself finally turn to look at the commotion, and my eyes met the steely blue eyes of one of the guards. He had been looking directly at me. Glancing at the rest, I saw they were all looking at us, eyes focused.

"Damn it." I rose to my feet, yanking Calum with me.

Their eyes widened, and one of them shouted, "Stop!"

They began to race toward us, moving as quickly as they could while weaving between the chairs.

My eyes flicked around the room in panic to try and find an exit but there was none. There was only one thing left to do.

I grabbed my sword, but before I could fully pull it out of its sheath, they were upon us.

"Calum!" I yelled as I heard her scream. They had grabbed us, and there was one on each of my arms, holding them firmly behind my back. Another pulled my sword free and stepped back.

I struggled the best I could, and only for a few seconds. I got an arm free before they grabbed it again. I tried to kick out, but a soldier struck my knee hard, and a fast zing of pain flared up my leg, immediately stilling me.

The crowd around us was yelling and stumbling as they tried to get out of the way, but the fight was over before it even began. I was not nearly as strong as these men, and there was no competition.

Soon they held us both firmly in place, and the room quieted.

"Move," a soldier behind me rumbled.

And before I had the chance to, they shoved me forward, making me stumble, and they hurriedly walked me out the door and into the night.

Calum was right behind me, and only one guard was holding her. Her face clenched at the pain of his grip, and my heart raced in anger.

"Please, we've done nothing wrong. You have the wrong people. Please," I stammered, but the soldiers didn't even glance at me.

A male voice rose from the darkness as my eyes adjusted. "I'm afraid not."

We were brought to a stop in the middle of the street, side by side, facing the voice.

It took my eyes a moment, but then I saw them. There was a ring of about twenty soldiers before us, blocking any escape. Behind them was a black caged wagon. It was a prisoner transport wagon with metal bars, open to the elements. There was no hiding in that, no safety. There were horses secured to it and about ten more horses for soldiers to ride.

For someone who had never seen a real army before, it looked like one. It was a show of power, a show of force.

"You are actually exactly who we've been looking for," he continued, stepping forward. He was obviously the one in charge, and he was older than the rest. I guessed he was in his fifties, but he was well-built, still a man of war. He wore a uniform similar to the uniforms of those he commanded, but he wore several medals and a slightly different emblem on his shoulder. Instead of the normal blue, his was red.

When his eyes landed on mine, my gut became squeamish. There was something there, something in his eyes that immediately made me uneasy. His eyes spoke of violence, and they spoke of purpose.

I tried to plead our case. "Please, sir, we've done nothing wrong."

Instead of responding, he smiled and reached into his pocket. He pulled out a piece of paper and unfolded it. I recognized it immediately, and he took the few steps between us, closing the distance, and held the paper up in front of me for me to see.

There was Calum. It was a picture of her face, hand-drawn. It was her. There was no doubt. It shocked me, and then confounded me. There was no way this was possible. Maybe it was some kind of magic. No, it couldn't be. We were in the real world and out of the Dark Forest. I had no answer.

"I have no doubt in my mind we have the right person." The man smirked as he lowered the picture. Then, he nodded to two of his men. They stepped forward with heavy chains in their hands.

"Please, please don't do this," I stammered, panic flooding my veins.

THE THINGS OF NATURE

The soldier holding the chains spoke. "General, do you want both of them or just her?"

He turned to me, eyed me, then nodded. "Both."

I felt a small amount of relief at that. At least we would be together.

Then, they slapped the chains on us. The metal was cold and it squeezed my wrists. Lifting my hands before me, I felt their immense weight.

When I looked over at Calum, her face was ashen with shock. Her eyes darted around her with fear, but she said nothing as they clamped the chains on her small wrists.

"Please, sir, General, we've done nothing wrong," I spoke softer, pleading.

"I am fully aware you've done nothing wrong."

My eyes widened in shock at his words and confusion rolled through me, but he continued. "I just like to catch the problems before they occur."

He turned then and spoke to Calum. "Any funny business and your friend here dies."

And with that, he turned and walked away without another glance, and we were left to stumble toward our cage.

It didn't take long to reach the palace. The cobblestones vibrated the carriage, and the cold metal bit into my wrists with the movement. I had no idea what was going on. Calum looked to be in a daze of disbelief and shock. As we were chained, standing, to either side of the cage, she was in front, and I in the back—it was impossible to speak to her or comfort her.

I wanted to tell her that everything would be okay. I wanted to tell her that we would find a way out. But none of that might be true. The only thing I'd be able to comfort her with would be lies, and I didn't have the heart for that. The truth was that I had no idea if we would be killed, imprisoned, or set free.

We came to a jarring halt in front of the palace which made both of us stumble where we stood. The guards came around back and opened the door, pulling both of us out. I was almost unable to catch myself as they yanked me to the ground.

Even though our circumstances were dire, it was hard not to notice the magnificence of the palace inside the gates. We could see the lush gardens stretching on for about a quarter of a mile between the gates and the palace front steps where we stood. There were miniature hedge mazes, fountains, and all the fruit trees you could imagine. The path inside the gates was made from crushed white stone instead of the cobblestones outside, and the gates themselves were tall, black, wrought iron, twisted and curled to look like vines and leaves.

The palace itself was white, from the front steps to the tallest tower. Most of the windows stretched upward several stories and were made of stained glass of every color imaginable. The roof tiles were slate gray and the blue flag of Amartoth flapped in the wind above every tower.

That place was jarringly stunning. There was a great deal of wealth, and I knew it was from the ridiculous quantities of trade throughout the Central Kingdom. That city was the center of everything, hence its name, and I understood then what wealth looked like.

We were pushed, or in Calum's case, half carried up the thirty steps to the front doors. The doors were as large as the rest of the palace, and it took several people to swing them open. Either these people did that all day long, or there were not many guests of the palace.

We were ushered inside, and I was struck again by the magnificence of the place.

Upon entering, we were in the throne room. The light coming in through the stained glass made the room gleam in rainbow colors. Behind the throne was the largest window I had ever seen, but that one was regular glass. It looked out onto a courtyard where we could just see the tops of more fruit trees. The regular light of day came in through that window and a few more in the ceiling.

The entire room was white, just like the outside, but it was dancing with color made of light. The throne was made of pure gold, and what sat there was most peculiar. When we approached, I was able to see that a boy sat on the throne, no more than twelve. He had startling blue eyes and a shock of blond hair. He wore several gold rings on his fingers. His clothes were white, neatly pressed. He was completely alone, and he looked down at us in confusion.

"My King," the General bowed slightly in recognition.

He then brought us forward to the base of the steps leading up to the throne. Placing his hands firmly on our shoulders, he shoved us down, so we were on our knees, side by side.

The young king spoke. "Who are they?"

His voice was small and hadn't deepened yet.

The General motioned to each of us. "This is the girl we've been hunting, My King, and this is her companion."

"Another witch?" the boy eyed Calum.

"Yes, My King," the General answered, then walked up the steps to speak to the King in private.

Two soldiers took his place behind us.

I had no idea how he could possibly have heard about Calum being a witch. Perhaps it had come from our village. But that was impossible. There was no way they could know she actually had powers. We had barely left the forest when the soldiers had come into the wanderers' camp. The village was the only explanation. Someone from the village must have come here with the information.

"I promise you, My King, she is the real deal this time. I have proof."

The General's voice echoed across the room even though he whispered. There was nothing in the room to dampen any noise.

The young king eyed Calum again. "Yes, but she doesn't look like a witch."

"My King, listen! I have told you before about these kinds of people!" The General's voice was raised enough that it was easy for all in the room to understand what he was saying.

The King shriveled back into his chair at the scolding, "I know, I know, she just doesn't look like one is all."

The child kept glancing at Calum who had eyes still filled with fear.

I wasn't sure what came over me then. I couldn't help but plead for our innocence. The King was obviously under the thumb of the General, but if I could convince him to let us go, then perhaps he would.

"Please, My King, we've done nothing wrong."

His eyes flicked to me then back to the General.

He sat forward a little in his chair, gaining a little bit of confidence and questioning, though there was still a little bit of fear lingering. "Wait . . . have they not done anything?"

For a moment, I thought the General might hit him, his fist clenching and unclenching at his side. He sighed deeply in exasperation, and his true colors bled through.

"You know nothing about witches, boy! It doesn't matter what she has done or hasn't done! You are still too young to understand these things!"

Anger flashed across the young king's face, but the General ignored that and instead turned to the soldiers gathered and the few servants waiting in the wings,

"None of you know what magic really is! It is evil—pure evil, a corruptive force."

He was right, at least about some witches. I remembered the witch from the woods. Though he was wrong about Calum. I knew Calum, and she would rather die than harm a living thing.

"She may look innocent now, but soon she will turn. It's not about what she has *done*, it's about what she *is*, and she is dangerous."

I thought that if only he knew her then he would know the truth. She wasn't dangerous and she never would be dangerous. The General was wrong. He was blind. He didn't know Calum.

"General!" the King leaned forward, anger on his own face.

The General slowly turned back to the young king as if he didn't quite believe what he had heard.

"You're overstepping your place," the King said more quietly. The boy eyed the General warily, unsure of how he would react.

"Well, I apologize, My King, if I have offended. I am merely telling the truth."

"Perhaps, but these people have done nothing wrong." The King's eyes turned back to Calum and that time they met. He had made up his mind.

"King, you know not of what you speak. I have proof this time, hard proof that she has magic. Listen to me! She is a real threat!"

"No! General, they've done nothing wrong!" the King repeated, and he looked so young, like a child defying his parents for the first time. There was fear in his eyes as well as determination.

The General stalked to stand directly in front of the boy, and before I could comprehend what was happening, he drew his sword. With one quick, perfect swipe, blood splattered the white tiles.

Chapter 16

The General—Forty Years Earlier

The child lay in his bed in the big house on the hill. He was only three. The sounds of the ocean wafted up through his open window, stirring the lace curtains and caressing his cheek. The night was deep and silent, punctuated with the sound of crickets. The only light came from the full moon and stars, which cast their silvery glow into the room and across his bed.

Then, that light began to change. The silvery glow began to mix with a warmer light. It came from the shore—soft, golden and red. It grew and then a bell clanged, waking the boy. Fire.

He sat up, eyes bleary, and stared out of the window. Smoke rose into the sky, illuminated by the bright flames.

THE THINGS OF NATURE

The houses along the water were engulfed, and the flaming tendrils wisped to one roof, then the next, bouncing upward from house to house.

As it spread closer, the sound of voices became clearer. There was yelling, screaming, but it all remained distant for the boy, a dream, as he watched it all happen, still far away.

Voices rose from down the hall, his parents. There was nothing to fear with his parents there. He was certain and unwavering in that like any young child would be. He had never feared before. He had never faced it as a rich merchant's son.

Then his door creaked open, and his mother tiptoed in, her nightgown feathery and wafting in the breeze from the open window.

"My child." She pulled him out of bed and held him in her arms. She gave him kisses and whispered, "I'm so sorry. I'm so sorry, sweetheart."

The boy remained silent, confused. He did not understand what was happening, so he closed his eyes and nestled into her neck, relishing her comfort, already falling back to sleep. But she sat him back down on the bed and pulled something silver and sparkling from her pocket. She tied it around his wrist, and he recognized the family crest, a small silver symbol.

"You must not take this off, do you understand?" She took the boy's hands and squeezed them firmly, begging him to pay attention.

The boy nodded, confused by the urgency in her tone.

Then she scooped him up and brought him to his wardrobe, opened it, shuffled some things aside, and placed him inside.

"You must not come out, no matter what you hear. You must stay here until the sun is back in the sky. Do you understand?"

The boy nodded in bewilderment and that seemed to reassure her.

"Alright, promise me. You will stay here."

"I promise," he spoke quietly, hesitantly.

She gripped the doors of the wardrobe, and her eyes drank in her son. Then, she was gone, the doors shut, and his world became dark.

As a child of three, it did not take him long to crack the door open. "Mom?" he half-whispered, half-called.

There was no response.

He then very slowly crept out. The light coming in through his window was brighter, and the smell of smoke wafted through the air.

Curious, he made his way back to the window and peaked over the edge.

There was fire everywhere, but it had not reached his house yet. There was a large yard separating theirs from the other houses, and it kept them safe from the reaching tendrils of flame.

Movement caught the boy's eyes. A person emerged from the burning town, but it was like no one the boy had ever seen before. The person wore a thick black robe with the hood drawn up. The boy could see none of their face, just their hands as one clutched what looked like a walking stick. But that stick was different. At the top of the stick was a glowing, red orb. It looked like a sphere of dancing flames.

As they neared the house, the boy's father stepped forward, into the boy's view, and the boy immediately felt relieved. His father was strong. His father would stand between that person and their home.

Before his father could speak, the stranger lifted their staff. Flame erupted from the sphere, cascading like water in giant, violent waves toward his father, and before the boy had time to blink, his father was engulfed. He heard his mother's scream, and he clapped his hands over his ears at the horrible sound.

For the first time, the boy was afraid. He ran back to the wardrobe and covered himself in clothes, closing the door behind him. His heart raced in panic and with one more scream from his mother, the air became silent but for the crackling of flames.

He stayed like that until the first rays of sun slid through the cracks in the wood. Then, very carefully, he made his way to the window once more. The village was gone. In its place was smoke and air. It was all burned away, and only black smudges remained.

His eyes landed on the smudges on the lawn, right in front of the house, and he felt something he had never felt before. A swirling of emotions cascaded inside of him—but most prominent was anger.

As the years passed, that anger sat inside of him, festering and growing. Born of grief, he rose with only anger as his guide.

Chapter 17

All I could see was a single drop of blood, as if in slow motion, drip from the General's sword. There was a moment of astonished silence, then there were screams from several of the servants in waiting, but soldiers grabbed them. Everything became chaos as soldier turned on soldier and some tried to flee.

I turned to Calum, and her face was crumpled up in horror and sorrow, a confusing mix of emotions like she had no idea what to feel. Then, she crumpled to the floor and passed out.

"Calum!" I tried calling to her, but she was motionless.

I reached out to her and shook her gently, then pulled her to me, not knowing what else to do. We had been forgotten in the commotion, and it became clear that most of the soldiers were on the General's side. There were only three that defied the larger group, and the room quieted as the servants were all rounded up to one side, and the three were left standing in the middle of the room.

It was only then that the General turned around. There was blood splattered across his cheek and his sleeve from his violence. As he eyed the room, he smiled. He had the upper hand, and my heart sank.

He spoke to the three. "Surrender."

And seeing as there was no way out, they slowly lowered their weapons to the floor. They were snatched up by the ones surrounding them, and the General smiled his first smile. He knew he had won, and the triumph and violence in his eyes said enough. We were not going to get out of anything.

"Kneel," he commanded again.

Everyone did as they were told, most willingly. Some of the servants were shoved to their knees, but they didn't rise or try to fight it. No one wanted to die.

Then, one of the other soldiers thumped his chest loudly with his fist and shouted, "My King!"

The rest followed suit, yelling as loudly as they could, "My King!" Thumping their chests in unison. Even the three soldiers who had fought at first knelt and joined in. They were less enthusiastic, but they did it nonetheless.

The General's eyes flicked back to us. "Put them in the dungeon."

Calum was ripped from my arms and I yelled in anguish, but there was nothing I could do. Two guards grabbed Calum by each of her armpits and dragged her behind me.

We were led to the left, out a side door, and down a hallway of lush red carpet. The walls wore gold and white wallpaper, and paintings adorned with golden frames hung every few feet. We made our way down several of these hallways, some with multiple doorways, some with only one. I soon became confused about which way we had come as every hallway looked the same. Then we came to a halt, and a guard opened one of the doors. A dark staircase spiraled downward, and I knew it must lead to the dungeon. It was probably a secret entrance from the royal living area.

We headed down, single file, and when we arrived at the bottom, the area opened. The first room held a few wooden tables and chairs that several prison guards sat at, relaxing. As we walked into the next room, the smell hit me. There were chains on the walls. You could tell they tried to keep the place clean, but blood coated the cracks in the floor. The guard keeping watch pulled out his keys and let us enter a locked door at the end of the room.

Doors to the cells were interspersed among the large stone walls. We couldn't see if there were any other prisoners, but I assumed there had to be.

One of the doors opened for me, and I was shoved inside. It was pitch-black, and I turned just in time to see Calum being dragged by as they closed my door.

"Calum!" I called out her name. The sound died immediately against the thick stones.

There was no way of knowing where they were taking her. It could be to the very next cell or to somewhere far away. I felt very much alone then, and I listened to the guards as they exited, walking back past my cell. When they were gone, there was silence, and it felt piercingly loud in the darkness where I sat with nothing but my own mind to haunt me. I thought about all the things they might do to us—what they already might be doing to Calum without my knowing. It ate at me, but all I could do was wait.

We should never have gone to the city. It was a mistake that could cost us our lives. There was nothing I could do but blame myself. I should have seen it coming or done something differentI should have known that they would still be looking for her or at least someone who looked like her. I couldn't understand how the picture could look so close to her. There was no one else on earth who knew her as well as I did. It made no sense how they could have been so accurate. The only explanation was that there was a very big piece missing from what I knew to be true, and what I knew was that I had been the only person Calum had interacted with since I had found her in those woods.

Either way, I had led her straight to one of the places we should have been running from, and the guilt sat heavily inside me.

It was many hours before a guard walked back down the row of cells. By then, my eyes had begun to grow accustomed to the dimness, and the cracks around the door let in just enough light that I could see my surroundings.

The floors, walls, and ceiling of the cell were made of huge slabs of stone. Shackles were attached to the wall in the corner. They were untouched, thankfully. I must not have been much of a threat.

The guard stopped in front of my door, and a small flap opened, letting a tray slide through. It was food, but it smelled fermented. Inspecting it closer, I could see the chunk of bread was moldy, and whatever was in the bowl was some kind of chunky mess. I couldn't eat it. I pushed the tray away from me with a clatter.

"Adric?" I heard Calum's voice, so faint I thought I might be imagining it.

"Calum?" I called, looking around frantically, but of course, she wasn't in my cell.

"Adric?" Her muffled voice came through the cracks in the wall to my left. I crawled over and her voice grew louder as we continued to call back and forth.

"Calum, are you hurt?"

There was a hesitation, then, "No, I just woke up here."

I felt myself sigh with relief. She had been beside me the whole time.

"Are you hurt?" she called back tentatively.

"No, I'm fine. They brought us straight down here, right after you passed out."

There was additional silence before she answered, "I'm sorry, Adric. This is all my fault. I convinced you that we should come here."

My heart stuttered at her words. "No! Calum! If anything, it's my fault. I am the one who brought you here. Besides, how could we know that this would happen?"

Another silence and then, "That's true."

"Either way, at least we're still together."

I heard her sigh in relief. "Yes, at least there's that."

We sat in the darkness for what felt like an eternity. More meals came and went, and days must have passed, but there was no telling in the darkness of the dungeon. My hunger eventually won, and I did my best to swallow some of the food given to us. It was rancid, and as time passed, I could feel myself growing weak just sitting there with hunger. They were probably trying to wear us down. I wasn't sure.

The General was also probably busy with his new duties as king. I imagined that there were a lot of people that needed convincing.

All we could do was wait and that was what we did.

Chapter 18

The General sat on the throne. Many still referred to him by that name; in their eyes, the boy was still their king. Even with the boy-king dead, the General did what he always had done, and that was to run the kingdom. He had held the King in the palm of his hand up until the night the boy's life had ended.

The transition was easy for the General, and he demanded tithes and gifts from other kings and merchants to prove their loyalty.

The doors opened, and the next person bearing gifts entered.

The man was perhaps thirty. It was hard to tell. He appeared youthful, but also experienced and physically well-toned. He stood at six feet. He had dark hair that fell into his eyes, and he wore all dark clothes to match. His servant walked slightly behind him, carrying a small chest.

The servant was even younger and shorter with soft brown hair.

"My King." The dark figure bowed at the base of the steps, and his servant followed his example.

"Now, what's your name so we can check you off the list?" the General asked, leaning toward his new adviser who held a very large list and quill.

"I am afraid I'm probably not on any of your lists, My King. You see, I am rather new to my wealth." He smiled and then added for emphasis, "Very new."

"I see." The General eyed him, but he wasn't about to turn anyone bearing gifts away.

"Give us your name anyway," he continued. "So we can at least add you to the list."

"My name is Reuben Hekking, My King." He bowed once more, smiling a friendly smile.

The General eyed him again warily. "That is a strange name."

"It is, My King. My apologies."

"There's no need to apologize, now what did you bring?"

The General got straight to the point, and Reuben nodded, motioning for his servant to come forward. The young man stepped up and opened the small chest, and the room sparkled with refracted light. Inside the chest were the most delicately cut gems in the world. They were all different colors and each the size of a thimble. The light hit them, and they sparkled in a million little bits.

The General's eyes widened, and his breath caught in his throat, but he composed himself.

The General had another question. He was interested in gaining more of these fine jewels. "This is a fine gift, son. Where did these gems come from?"

The General's greed was a potent thing.

"From my mine, My King. That's how I came into such wealth so quickly."

The General leaned forward in his chair, very interested. If that was the owner of the mine, then perhaps a new friendship was in order. With wealth came power, so having someone like that on his side was of the utmost importance.

The General smiled. "Well, Reuben, I am sure you are weary from your travels. You must stay here for the night. I insist."

Reuben bowed, smiling a secret smile of his own. "Of course, My King."

The chest was handed over, and they were ushered out of the room to the guest chambers.

The adviser looked at the General incredulously. He did not understand the decisions of the General, but every move was played carefully, like a game of chess. Power was hard to get but even harder to maintain. He had played that game all his life, and he knew what moves to make.

⋆⊷⊶◉◉⊷⊶⋆

The General was happy with a good day's work, and he thought he might reward himself with a little visit to the dungeon. What was held down there was important, and he had waited long enough. Hopefully, they were ready to talk.

As he reached the basement, the soldiers stood in surprise, pounding their chests and saying, "My King!" to show their allegiance.

As the General, it had been easy to obtain their loyalty, and once someone had an army, there was no stopping them.

The General was given a torch and led down the line of cells.

"Which one, My King?" The soldier pulled out the keys.

"The boy," he answered.

He didn't wish to fool around with the one bearing magic quite yet. She was just too dangerous, and even though she didn't look like it, there was probably violence in her heart.

The door swung open, and the General stepped forward with his torch raised.

The boy sat at the back of his cell. There was dirt and grime on his skin, and he stank. His eyes squinted at the sudden intrusion of light, but he didn't move, too tired and worn.

"Are you ready to talk, boy?" the General questioned, placing the torch in its holder by the door.

The boy recognized his voice and stiffened slightly. "What do you want to know?"

The General crouched before the boy.

"Where did she get her magic?" he asked.

The boy looked almost confused by the question. "Well . . . I didn't even know she had magic until a week ago. But it was always inside of her. Technically, she's always had it. It's a part of her."

The General did not like that answer. He cracked his knuckles and then his neck. "That doesn't make any sense. She had to get it somewhere."

The boy frowned. "The witch in the forest told her where to find it inside of herself and how to use it."

"Which forest?"

"The Dark Forest."

The General scoffed. "Sure."

He didn't believe the boy at all. No one ever went into the Dark Forest. No one. The boy was lying. He had to be.

You see, the General knew something that the boy didn't know, and he smiled with the knowledge he was about to share. "There is no use lying to me, boy. For I know that her parents do not possess any kind of magic. Therefore, she couldn't have been born with it. She had to have found it somewhere. Where?"

The boy simply looked at the General, stunned, the gears in his brain spinning.

"How do you know about her parents?"

"I have a reliable source." The General continued to smile.

The boy kept his mouth shut, not sure then how much the General really knew. Perhaps he was lying. As far as the boy knew, there was no one else who had known of Calum's existence except himself before their journey had begun. Maybe he had been wrong. He had no idea of what had happened to Calum before they had met. He had never thought it important to know.

He then second-guessed himself, and the uncertainty sat heavy upon his heart.

The General changed the subject, knowing that he had just told the boy a truth that had hit him hard. "There is something else I need to know, boy. Where are the others?"

"The others?"

The General rolled his eyes. "Yes, the others you were traveling with."

"No one came here with us," the boy responded.

He was telling the truth, but only part of the truth.

The General knew it.

He leaned forward onto the balls of his feet, his face coming closer to the boy's. "I know you're lying. You forget that I am the General, the King. I have eyes everywhere. How do you think I made it this far? You have to be cunning, smart. I needed to outsmart my opponent. I know you had companions; you were all seen together in that camp. I also know that those companions were deserters, at least a few of them. Their swords were army-issued weapons. Now, who were they?"

The boy looked the General in the eyes, and he clamped his lips shut. His eyes hardened in determination. He wasn't going to speak anymore. But the General didn't care. He had more up his sleeve, and he was sure the boy would speak in the end.

He sighed and stood. If he couldn't get information out of the boy by speaking to him reasonably, then he was going to have to take some more drastic measures, and he knew just where to find them.

Chapter 19

I felt my chest loosen in relief as I was enveloped in darkness once more. The General was gone, taking the light with him, and he left me in the musty stink of my cell, by then familiar.

My mind spun in confusion. The General did indeed know a lot. He knew about the others back at the wanderers' camp, and he somehow knew about Calum. Maybe he was lying about her parents, but that didn't fit into everything else. So far, he had told me the truth. The rest of his questioning had been sound, all except for that. Maybe his source was wrong. I had no idea who his source was anyway. It was probably the same source that had drawn the perfect picture of Calum, the one they had all used to find her.

"Adric?" Calum's soft voice rose from the wall that stood between us.

THE THINGS OF NATURE

I crawled back over to my usual spot. "I'm here, Calum."

"Are you alright?"

"Yes, I'm fine. He was just talking to me."

"I heard," she confessed, and silence stood like the wall between us.

"Did you hear what he said?" I finally asked.

"I did."

"About your parents?" I prodded.

Her response was so quiet it was almost impossible to hear. "I don't remember anything before you."

My eyes widened. "You don't remember anything before me? Nothing at all?"

She had never wanted to tell me anything before, but I had thought it was too painful. I had never assumed she had forgotten or couldn't remember.

"Nothing," she answered.

Well, that explained why she had always avoided my questions.

Perhaps she had blocked it out. I had heard of that happening with soldiers coming home from war. They had lived through a traumatizing experience, and their brain had blocked out all the memories, but that didn't quite fit with Calum. It made me think. Maybe her past was traumatic. I felt an uneasiness in my gut, but it eased as I realized at least she hadn't been lying to me. She hadn't kept secrets from me. She was still who I always knew her to be.

I tried to reassure her through the wall. "We'll figure it out, Calum."

She didn't answer, and I hoped she was okay. She was probably feeling guilty about being unable to remember. At that point, the General had the upper hand. He knew things we didn't unless he was lying. But by the look in his eyes, I didn't think he was.

I made my way back over to my spot and several hours, or at least what felt like several hours, passed. I knew it was almost time for a meal tray to be slid through the slot, but instead of one pair of boots coming down the hall, I heard several.

The door to my cell opened once more, and the General entered. The light blinded me again, and I couldn't see who was behind him. There was definitely someone there.

The door closed behind both of them, and the General stepped forward. "I've brought someone to see you, an old friend."

Old friend? My mind immediately went back to the village, but there was no one I could possibly think of. I had lived on the edge of civilization for a reason, and unless it was one of our new friends from the Dark Forest, then there was no one else.

"Hello, Adric." The figure stepped forward, and I recognized that voice. It couldn't be.

He took one more step forward and the light of the torch shone on his face.

"Lucian?"

His eyes were hard, and he looked upon me with disgust. He looked more worn and skinnier than I remembered, but it was definitely him. There were dark circles under his eyes, and he looked as if he were haunted by something.

"Of course," he responded with bitterness in his tone.

I was so confused. He must have come all the way from the village just to tell them about Calum. But he couldn't be the source. He was the one who had spotted her and told the villagers about her, though. It seemed so far-fetched. I couldn't fathom why someone would listen to him. The man I knew had no brain between his ears. The only thing he had ever enjoyed was teasing other kids in our one-room schoolhouse or causing trouble. Even though he was several years younger than me, his behavior still bothered me. He had always been a poor student, and he had been a worse adult, drinking and trolling around with his friends. I didn't know why they'd believe anything he said.

"This young man here," the General patted Lucian on the shoulder, "is the one who brought me proof of the witch."

"Proof? What proof?" I questioned. It was insane. There was no way.

Lucian stepped forward and looked back at the General for permission.

The General gave it, nodding. Then, Lucian reached for the sleeve of his shirt, rolling it up to his elbow. There was nothing on his skin that I could see. There were no marks or anything, just him. I looked up into his eyes in confusion, and he pointed to his wrist, annoyance dripping from his mouth.

"The bracelet."

I hadn't thought anything of the small bracelet around his wrist, but looking closer, I could see it was green.

"You're going to have to step closer," I said.

Lucian's eyes hardened more.

He shoved his wrist into my face.

Then I understood. The bracelet was magic.

There was a single blade of grass wrapped around his wrist, fresh and alive, no more than half a centimeter wide. No clasp or anything held it around his wrist. It was a never-ending blade that did not begin or end, and poking out of that single blade were the smallest white daisies I had ever seen. Their petals uncurled, and they were in perfect condition. There were only four of them on the blade, but they were simple, beautiful.

It led me to more questions. Calum did have the power of nature, but she hadn't found her magic until the Dark Forest. Maybe it had been someone else. That didn't make much sense either. Someone like Calum had to be rare. If it really was her, then I had no idea when this could have happened. The only time that made sense was if it happened before we met. If Calum made the bracelet before we met, then she must have known Lucian from her life before, and that was a terrifying thought.

"Did Calum give that to you?" I questioned, eyeing him.

I had known Lucian all my life, and I felt like I would know if he was lying.

"She did, when we were kids," he answered.

I continued my interrogation. "Kids? That was a long time ago. You've never taken it off?"

It should have fallen off by now, shriveled up, and died.

Lucian huffed out a laugh.

"It doesn't *come* off." He hooked his finger through it and yanked, hard. I expected there to be no resistance, but there was; the bracelet stayed on and looked completely undamaged by the attempt.

"I've tried many, many times to get it off. I've been trying to forget—to forget *her*. But I can't with this thing on my wrist."

He rolled back down his sleeve.

The thing was magic. There was no doubt about that.

"And you're sure it was Calum?" I asked; I felt my heart sink.

There was just too much I didn't know about her past, and it was putting us at a disadvantage I didn't even know we had. I felt myself losing the battle.

"It was definitely Calum."

"How can you be sure?"

I hoped in the deepest part of me that he didn't have any hard evidence.

He leaned down so our faces could be closer, and his eyes flared with anger. "She's my sister."

<hr />

She was his sister. I didn't want it to be true. It couldn't be true. When I had found her in the woods, she had been so young. But it made sense that she couldn't have gotten far. I had guessed that she had run from somewhere nearby and that was why I had kept her so well hidden. She hadn't been in good shape either when I had stumbled across her. Whoever she had run from had hurt her. After I had found out about her magic, I assumed they had probably found out about her gifts and had run her out in fear like the villagers had done to us.

These thoughts swirled through my brain. I couldn't believe it. If he was truly her brother, then why would he turn her in? He would have had to walk across half the kingdom just to do it. That was more effort than I had ever known him to make.

"Why?" I asked, trying to understand. "Why would you do this?"

"Oh, Adric," he taunted. "You really don't know Calum at all, do you?"

Frustration blossomed inside of me. I did. I did know her. We had been through thick and thin together. We were going to build a new life together. I knew who she was, and what kind of person she was.

"You're wrong," I answered.

And at my response, the anger flared new in his eyes. "No, Adric, you don't. You don't know what she did to me. You don't know anything about her. Did you know that the day she left, she left me with *them*? She left me, alone and scared, with those *people* who call themselves our parents. I will never forgive her for that, ever."

My heart sank once more. The one thing I assumed deep down was that she hadn't just left. She had run away, and I was pretty sure she had run out of desperation.

"I don't think she meant to leave you, Lucian," I replied softly.

He scoffed. "I don't care if she meant to or not, Adric. What matters is that she *did*. She could have taken me with her, and instead, she left me."

I then understood where all that anger inside of him was coming from. He believed that Calum had left him behind, betraying him. But they had only been children back then, and she had been scared. It seemed pretty clear to me what had occurred, but Lucian was so caught up in his own wrath that he didn't see.

I also finally understood why he had done what he had done back at the village. He must have recognized her, and his anger had overtaken him. Then, once he found out we had escaped, he must have drawn her from memory and had come to the city for assistance. Coming to Amartoth, he had found the General who had been all too eager to help.

"Alright." The General stepped forward, bored of the conversation. "I hope this helps you to understand, Adric, how serious I am. You are going to give me answers whether you like it or not, and I will know if you're lying."

The General patted Lucian's arm and pulled him back toward my cell door where Lucian glared at me one last time before departing.

The moment the cell door closed, and I heard the footsteps dissipate down the hall, I crawled back over to the wall between me and Calum.

"Calum, I'm so sorry. Is he really your brother? Do you remember?"

The questions flowed out of me, and I had to restrain myself from letting even more loose. I didn't want to overwhelm her, and I was sure she already had plenty to think about.

Instead of answering, I could only hear some soft noises, small gasps for air and sniffling.

She was crying.

"Calum, are you okay? I'm so sorry." I felt my heart break at the sounds of her sobs as they filtered through the rock. I could almost see her trying to cover up the noise, but there was no stopping it.

Then she spoke, her voice coming to me between gasps for air. "Adric . . . I can't believe . . . I left him. I'm such a . . . terrible person."

"Calum, I'm sure you didn't mean to."

"But I d-did," she stammered, and I took a deep breath.

"Listen, Calum. That day that I found you? I can remember it as clearly as if it were yesterday. When I came out of the woods and into the clearing, you had been scared. I remember the look on your face. You had been terrified. You ran away for a reason. You were running from something. I'm sure you only left him behind because you had no choice."

"Really?"

"Yes, really."

I sat with her as the sniffles subsided. It was several minutes before she spoke again.

"I think . . . I think I'm remembering a little bit. They're flashes and images, but I think I'm starting to remember."

"That's good, Calum! I'm sure it will keep coming back to you," I answered.

I wished I could reach through the wall and hold her, reassure her. I felt so distant and removed from her, but it was not like there was anything I could do. I just hoped that she would remember everything soon and remove the upper hand that the General had over us.

Chapter 20

The General led Lucian up through the castle, his hand holding his upper arm as if he were afraid Lucian might bolt. But he had nothing to worry about. Lucian was exactly where he wanted to be.

They passed through halls and moved toward the back of the castle, walking by an armory, swords and old armor littering the walls from old wars. They exited the back of the castle into the sunshine. Birds chirped sweetly from the trees, and insects buzzed from flower to flower. To the left stood the royal stables, filled with the mightiest creatures on the continent. Farther forward, past more gardens, stood the low buildings of the barracks which only stood three stories tall. The royal militia lived there, guarding the castle and city.

That was where they headed, and several guards milled about outside, smoking and enjoying the fresh spring air. By then, the leaves on the trees were all out, and fresh grass was thick on the ground.

Heading inside, they came to the General's office, which he had already decided to maintain as his own. Even if he was king, there was always danger in giving someone else any bit of power. This way, he could keep the duties and power of the General while also being king. That was how he had gotten there, after all.

He sat Lucian in a chair in front of his desk, and he sat facing him in his tall-backed chair.

"I gave you a promise. If you wish, I will enroll you now in training. It was the royal guard you wanted, correct?"

Lucian nodded vigorously. "Yes, please."

"Good." The General made a note in the ledger on his desk with his quill.

Then his eyes flicked up, and a smile appeared on his lips. "There's just one thing you have to do in order to enter the institute."

"What is it? Whatever it is, I'll do it."

"It's one final test, a test of loyalty," the General conceded.

Lucian smiled in turn. "Can we do it now, or do I have to wait?"

He had no issue performing any task the General set out. Becoming a royal guard meant good food and housing, and he could finally be somebody. Perhaps he could even be a general someday.

But he didn't know the General. If he was in power, he was going to do anything to maintain that power. No one would be rising that far up in his ranks. He was going to maintain control, and that meant no one could question his authority.

For the General, giving Lucian the position was of little consequence. He was becoming another soldier in the multitude.

And technically, there was no test of loyalty. The General had completely made it up. He wanted to have a little fun. Since he was king, he wanted to enjoy it while it lasted.

"We can do it today if you wish," the General answered.

Lucian smiled. "I would like to do it as soon as possible."

Little did Lucian know what the General had planned. He had not seen the General's true nature. The General's games were anything but fun, and Lucian would soon regret all the decisions he had ever made to get him to where he was that day.

They met at the back entrance to the castle. Lucian wore new clothes, the clothes of a soldier in training with the royal insignia on his sleeve. The General had gifted it to him, and it simply boosted Lucian's confidence. With the uniform he was somebody, and it made him sure that he would pass the test easily.

The General led him back through the castle, and Lucian recognized the way. "Are we going back to the dungeon?"

"We are."

"Why?" Lucian persisted.

"You'll find out soon enough."

Lucian sighed but let the General lead him back to the dungeon.

Upon arriving, they entered the second room, which contained the chains and blood in the cracks of the floor. It was the interrogation room.

The General motioned to the soldier standing guard. "Bring them out."

The soldier nodded and disappeared down the hall, another following behind.

Silence passed, and then there was the sound of chains. Calum was brought out first. She blinked against the bright torches and stumbled, her feet unsteady from hunger and tiredness. The soldier brought her to the center of the room, then pushed her to her knees, and she let out a soft gasp at the impact. She was dirty, her hair wild, and she looked tormented, her eyes red as if she had been crying.

Lucian's eyes widened at the sight of her. Her appearance took him off guard. It had been a long time, and she looked small, weak.

Next came Adric. He also blinked against the brightness, and the soldier behind him kicked at the back of his legs to bring him to his knees. His eyes widened in recognition of Calum kneeling by his side.

"Calum," he started with concern written all over his face.

"Quiet," the General commanded, and Adric closed his mouth, but his eyes continued to flick back to Calum's face.

Calum merely looked at Lucian, her eyes searching his face for something.

Lucian stood to the side, observing. He wasn't sure what was happening at that point. He had done as the General had told him. He had shown Adric his proof of what Calum was, and he had revealed who he was to Calum. He wasn't sure what the General had in mind.

Actually, having Calum in front of him had made him momentarily forget his rage. Her eyes were large and afraid. She was fully grown, but she was still exactly the same. She was the adorable little sister with crazy hair and doe eyes.

The General turned to Lucian. "This is your test. Come here."

Lucian stepped forward, and the General pulled out his golden sword.

"As a soldier, you will have to do as you're commanded without question, even if you don't understand or agree." The General spoke and held out his sword.

Lucian's eyes widened, but he took it. The sword was heavy in his hands, made of hard steel with a handle made of gold. It was the sword of a king.

"This is your task. Kill her."

The General stepped back, a look of satisfaction on his face he couldn't hide. He wasn't sure what would happen. Either way, it would be entertaining.

"No!" Adric shouted. "You can't!"

Panic radiated through Adric's eyes as Lucian stepped forward, taking in one deep breath after another as if he were trying to steady himself, but there was nothing Adric could do between his chains and the guard holding him down.

This was Adric's worst nightmare. He was completely helpless.

Lucian stepped forward to stand in front of Calum, gripping the sword now in his right hand. But when he raised his eyes to meet hers, he paled. He could almost feel her fear as it radiated off her.

"Sir," Lucian hesitated. "I know you just said not to question you, but I'm not sure if there's a point to this."

Seeing her again for the first time had jarred him. She was innocent and afraid. It was impossible to imagine someone as genuine as Calum being evil. There was no malice in her eyes, only sadness and shame at what she had done.

The General scoffed. "She is a witch, Lucian. She is dangerous. There was never any other option for her."

Lucian continued to hesitate. Their eyes searched each other's as if they were communicating, and Lucian battled within himself. His emotions were all over the place, but then he seemed to find resolve, and he lifted the sword. She had betrayed him, left him, and had never come back. "You left me, Calum. There's no excuse."

The anger from before surged back, the surprise from seeing her again for the first time gone.

Adric tried to stall him. "Don't do it, Lucian."

"Quiet," the General snarled again.

Calum's eyes then flicked to Adric's. Lucian ground his teeth, determination filling him. He told himself he could do it, that he just needed to remember what she had done to him; and he let the anger that had filled him for so many years remind him.

Then Calum spoke, her soft voice rising through the room. "Lucian." She took in a shaky breath, and her voice was barely a whisper. "Do it quickly, okay?"

Lucian's eyes widened in surprise. He hadn't expected her to speak. Her voice was older, but again, it was the same.

"Make it quick." Her eyes looked into his, pleading and understanding. She only cared for him. She held nothing against him. She took the guilt she felt and let it flow through her.

Lucian was frozen.

"Calum, stop!" Adric looked at her in disbelief, but he understood what she was trying to do.

She wanted to make it easier for Lucian. She wanted him to know that she understood. She felt bad for leaving him and, therefore, took on the cloak of guilt.

The General stepped forward, and a loud clap resounded through the room as he slapped Adric across the face, almost sending him backward to the ground. "You are here to watch, nothing more."

Adric clamped his mouth shut, dazed.

Calum began to speak again. "Lucian . . . Brother . . ."

"SHUT UP!" Lucian screamed, making everyone jump. He had been a statue, but now the rage exploded out of him. "You're a witch, Calum! You're evil! You deserve this, after everything you've done!"

Calum shook her head. "No, Lucian. Magic is good! It's a gift."

"You're wrong, Calum. It's a curse. It's not something you can control!"

Those words reminded Adric of what the General had said before about magic. It was almost word for word.

She shook her head again. "You should know, of all people, that it's good. I remember now. I remember everything."

Her eyes were then soft, and although there was still guilt, there was sorrow also.

Seeing Lucian standing before her after so long, and having looked him in the eyes, her memories had come flooding back. Their connection had waned after so many years, but with that one look into his eyes, into his heart, she had remembered.

"You remember leaving me now? I wasn't aware you had forgotten," Lucian spat back. His own eyes were sharp with blame.

"Yes, Lucian," she answered. "I ran away. I had no choice. They found out I had magic. I think *you're* the one that is not remembering clearly."

His eyes hardened and his teeth ground together.

Her eyes bore into his.

"Do you not recall how they hurt me, Lucian? They were afraid of me. They were going to hand me over to some strangers. I broke free, and I ran. I never looked back. I couldn't come back, and I knew you were safe. I remember now how scared you were. I remember you watching as they dragged me away. I watched as you pushed your gift deep down, burying it inside where it could never come out."

"What are you talking about?" Lucian's voice lowered, confused.

"You buried your gift, Lucian. You forgot about it. You saw what they did to me, and you hid."

"I have no clue what you're talking about," Lucian replied. His anger dissipated somewhat as confusion took over.

"Yes, you do. You have a gift, too. It's not something to be scared of, Brother. Let me show you."

She reached out her chained hand to his, and before he could move away, she touched his skin.

Lucian's eyes widened, and energy flowed between them as Calum let her gift wash over him. She was reaching into him, searching deep inside him like she had done to find her own gift. When she found what she was searching for, his eyes slowly began to glow. It was soft at first, then grew, just like Calum's eyes when the witch had awoken her power. His irises turned red-hot as if they were on fire. They were like a molten, rolling lava of flame and darkness, twisting and igniting. Then he closed his eyes, remembering.

Everyone was still in surprise for several minutes as Lucian breathed in deeply, and Calum's hand remained on his.

When he opened his eyes again, the light was gone, and so was the anger. The memories had flooded back, and in place of the anger, there was just disbelief and shock at the revelation. "I forgot. How did I forget?"

"You were protecting yourself. It's not your fault," she murmured, and tears began to track their way down her cheeks. What they had shared was intimate, and remembering their childhood so clearly brought back all those feelings from so long ago.

He sighed. "Calum, I'm sorry."

Before he could say anything else, the General stepped forward. "Is this true? Do you have magic?"

He drew his dagger from his hip and pointed it at Lucian, who quickly swiveled, raising his sword to protect himself. His eyes widened as he realized the immediate danger.

Calum's hand dropped away.

"No." Lucian denied it, but the denial was halfhearted.

The General barked out a laugh. "I saw the glow coming out of your eyes, Lucian. I should have realized it."

He pointed his dagger at Lucian and then Calum.

"You're related. You probably got your magic from the same place."

Lucian's breathing quickened as he began to panic. He didn't really know how to use the sword he had been given.

The General continued, "I'm sorry, Lucian. You must understand that I can't have anyone running around with magic, no matter who they are."

Then he lunged forward, his dagger flashing in the torchlight.

Chapter 21

The General lunged forward and aimed directly at Lucian's chest.

In absolute panic, Lucian dropped the sword with a loud clatter and grabbed for the dagger. Both of his hands wrapped around the blade, stopping it just before it entered his stomach. Blood began to drip from the cuts in his palms.

The General hissed in annoyance and tried to pull the dagger back, but Lucian held onto it firmly, even with the blade slick with blood.

A moment passed as the General yanked again. Lucian held firm, his eyes turning from fear to determination. He had forgotten who he was. He was remembering the shame and the fear of magic from when he was a child. He had pushed his magic so far down he had forgotten himself in the process. Calum had reminded him of what they had. He remembered the care and the love between them before her magic had been discovered. He remembered them playing together with their magic, behind their parents' backs. He remembered those intimate moments, and he remembered himself. He remembered what was truly important to him. Calum. He remembered her kindness and her smiles. He remembered her love and attention, the only kindness he had ever known. It had all come back to him in a flood, and it flowed through his veins.

His eyes began to glow red once more, wisps of red power escaping from his irises. The General hissed in pain and let go of the dagger, which sang with heat. Molten metal dripped between Lucian's fingers and splattered to the floor in red-hot droplets.

The General stepped away in fear, but after glancing around, his eyes landed back on his sword. He lunged forward and grabbed it. He turned and pointed it at Lucian, the final drop of molten metal leaving his fingers and falling to the floor with a hiss.

The two guards behind Calum and Adric backed away at the display, eyes wide. Then they were gone, running in fear through the dungeon.

Lucian had a wild glint in his eyes, and Adric recognized it as the same expression he had seen back at the village when Lucian had been convincing everyone to go on that witch hunt.

"You were really going to make me kill my sister?"

"She's a witch. She's evil," the General spat in response, saying the same thing he always had. His eyes were still strong and determined, but there was a new emotion just below the surface. There was fear; something the General hadn't felt in a long time.

"You want to see evil? I'll show you evil." Lucian smiled and stepped forward, his left hand bursting into flames.

The General's eyes widened and sweat began to form on his brow. Then Calum's shrill voice cut through the room. "Lucian! Stop! Don't kill him! You'll be exactly who he says we are."

Of course, Calum didn't want the General to die. She didn't wish harm upon anyone. She was in tune with nature, and seeing a life wink out would be devastating. She believed that everyone deserved a second chance, no matter who they were. In her eyes, death was never the answer.

Lucian shook his head. "Calum, I need to do this. He will never stop. He will never stop coming after us."

"Yes, but no one deserves death, Lucian. Let's just leave. Get us out of here, and we'll run!"

Lucian turned his eyes to Calum, aggravated. He was torn. He didn't want to refuse Calum anything, but the General had to go.

Adric watched her, too. He knew Calum to always have that kindness, but it was not the time for it. Lucian was right, the General would never stop. It was their only option.

In that moment of distraction, the General moved. Before anyone else had time to react, the General struck, his sword entering Lucian's chest, and it continued out his back, covered in red.

Lucian's flames flicked out in less than a second, and he was back to normal. His eyes snapped back to the General in surprise, and then his face crumpled in pain.

The General yanked his sword free, and Lucian fell to the floor. Blood dripped and began to pool, staining the dungeon floor.

"Lucian!" Calum cried and crawled as best she could to sit beside him.

The General looked on, satisfied that things were as they should be, but little did he know that Adric had moved.

Adric had been quiet, and he saw his chance the moment the General was distracted with his victory. He knew what had to be done. He reached forward and grabbed a chunk of the cooled metal from the floor. It was the only thing he could use as a weapon. It was still quite hot in his hands, but he could hold it for a few seconds. He rose on shaky legs and took the few steps to come up behind the General. He raised the chunk of metal over his head as quietly as he could with his chains, and he brought it down fiercely on the General's head.

The General crumpled to the ground, unconscious, and Adric let the chunk of metal slip from his fingers. He fell back to his knees in exhaustion and relief. It was the best he could do in his weakened state.

Lucian whispered, "Calum . . ."

She sobbed. "It's alright, Lucian. Everything is going to be okay. I'll fix you up."

She picked him up the best she could and laid his head in her lap. Lucian had eyes only for her, and his hand hovered over his chest, not sure what to do.

"Cal . . ." Lucian tried to speak, but Calum shook her head. "It's alright. Everything is going to be alright."

She placed her hand over his chest and squeezed her eyes shut, trying to concentrate. She stayed like that, lines of concentration on her face, her hand turning bloody from his wound. Tears sat on her eyelashes.

"I'm sorry, Calum," Lucian whispered, and blood trickled from the corner of his mouth.

She panicked. "No, no. It's not working! I don't know what to do!"

She didn't have the gift of healing, but she was trying anyway, hoping for a miracle.

"Calum," Adric spoke up, and her eyes opened, darting over to look at him. The look he gave her was one of devastation and grief. Looking at him, she realized there truly was nothing she could do. She saw his resignation and understood. You could be the most powerful person in the world, but there was no stopping death.

She turned back to Lucian. "I'm so sorry, Lucian. I've failed you so many times," she murmured and stroked his hair out of his eyes. Her guilt and sorrow swirled through her.

He shook his head ever so slightly. "None of it is your fault," he slurred, and his eyelids drooped. "I missed you," he murmured and closed his eyes, letting his hand fall back to his side.

He was fading quickly. With one last effort, he raised his hand to touch her cheek.

Then, he became unnaturally still, his final breath leaving him.

"No!" Calum shook him. "Lucian!" The floodgates broke and tears streamed down her cheeks.

Then Adric was there. "Calum, let go." He reached and took her hands in his, willing her to let him go. There was nothing she could do for him anymore. He was gone.

She released Lucian with a sob, but a moment later came back to place her hand on his cheek, leaving blood. "Brother," she whispered, her face twisting in grief.

She leaned forward, resting her forehead on his chest, and Adric placed his hand on her back, letting her know that he was there. With his touch, she looked up, and when her eyes connected with his, she threw her arms around him, burying her face in his chest.

She held him with all her strength as if she was afraid he would be gone in the next instant. He held her just as tightly, and he relished the moment. He was shaken, and it made him realize even more how much he cared for her.

A soft groan rose several feet away, and the General stirred. Adric's eyes snapped up, and he rose to his feet, bringing Calum with him.

"We need to go," he breathed into her hair.

She shook her head. "We can't leave him here." She sniffed.

"There's nothing we can do," Adric answered as he tried to pull her away again, but she stood firm.

"No. I think . . . I think there is actually something I can do."

She knelt a few feet away from him and placed her hands on the cold stones. She closed her eyes and took in a deep breath, letting it out slowly. The ground began to rumble, and dust fell from the rafters. It felt like the whole earth was shaking and it became so violent Adric had to grab the wall. Then, the stones around Lucian's body began to crack with the force. It appeared he might fall through the floor, but instead, vines began to wind their way out from the cracks, entwining and grabbing his body.

Soon, there was a churning mass of vines sprouting leaves and blue flowers. They covered the body, and they slowly sank back down into the earth, bringing Lucian with them. Once the body was completely in the ground, the soil rose back up, covering and concealing until there was just a dirt floor once more. The only evidence that anything had occurred was the mass of broken stones scattered about.

Chapter 22

We ran down hallway after hallway. I had Calum's hand in mine, and I pulled her along with me as we frantically ran one way, then the next.

We had found our way up the stairs and into the castle, but from there it was an endless maze of identical hallways, and we certainly stuck out. We both stank, covered in dirt and grime. Our clothes were also stained with dirt and filth, but there was nothing we could do about it.

All I could think was that I wanted out as soon as possible. The whole place felt like a trap, and even though we were out of the dungeons, it still felt like we were in a cage. I just wanted out. I wanted to get a breath of fresh air and feel the sun on my face. I felt almost desperate.

That desperation only rose as we ran, and the few windows we passed indicated that it was nighttime. The sun had just set, and the windows had turned from a soft gray to black.

Luckily, we hadn't run into anyone yet, but it was only a matter of time.

Then our luck ran out. I heard footsteps and voices coming around the next corner. They were still a distance away, but they were coming quickly.

Looking back down the hall, we didn't have enough time to make it back the way we had come, so I did the only thing I could think of to do. I grabbed the handle of the door beside us and tried it. Locked. I ran the few paces to the next one. Locked. Then the third. Locked.

I could hear them. They were almost around the corner. I tried the fourth door, and it opened easily into darkness. I tugged Calum inside and closed the door as softly as possible, making only the tiniest click. Air rushed out of me in relief. That was close.

Then I heard the lock clicking into place, and the room was suddenly filled with candlelight.

I turned, holding Calum close to my side, to face the guest room. Like in the hallway, there was plush red carpet. The walls were cream with gold trim and the rest of the room was as lavish with a dark wood desk, dresser, and washstand. The bed was huge, big enough for three to sleep comfortably, and it was also dark wood, covered in cream.

My eyes skimmed over all of it in an instant before landing on the source of the light. A lone candle flickered by the bed, and a dark figure stood behind it, holding it up.

"And who might you be?" His voice was deep, and he wore all black to match his hair.

His eyes narrowed, and he stepped forward to get a better look.

I grabbed the handle of the door and tried to open it, but it was indeed locked.

"We're nobody. Just forget we were here," I answered, and Calum gripped my arm.

The man took several more steps forward, and his eyes roved over us, taking in our dirty appearance, and his nose wrinkled at the smell coming off us.

"If you came from the dungeon, then I am extremely impressed." He came to stand before us, and I could tell that he didn't miss much. He was perceptive for realizing so quickly where we had come from, and his eyes spoke of holding a great deal of knowledge, similar to Her with the centaurs.

"Hold still a moment," he said and held out his candle, first toward me and then toward Calum.

"What are you doing?" I questioned, suspicious.

"Just getting a better look," he replied nonchalantly.

When the candle came to rest in front of Calum, it changed. The flame turned green, casting the whole room in a greenish glow.

The man grinned then, letting his teeth show. "Nature magic!"

My heart raced in surprise. I couldn't help but deny it. We were in enough danger as it was, and I wanted to get her out, get both of us out.

"What? No!"

Then the man held up a hand, making me pause. "I promise I intend to bring no harm to you. In fact, I intend to do the opposite. Darius!" he called over his shoulder.

Another man emerged from a side room, which I hadn't noticed previously, and he smiled. He was younger than the dark one, and he had striking blond hair. He was perhaps only a few years older than I.

"Is this one for real?" he asked upon seeing us.

Stepping forward, I noticed he was tired. There were slight bags under his eyes, and he looked annoyed.

The dark one turned on him, aggravated. "Darius! Are you serious?"

"I'm tired, in case you didn't notice. And, Reuben, in case you forgot, I'm the one who is pretending to be your servant! They have me doing all sorts of chores while you get to sit up here like a pretty princess! And I'm tired of doing all these rescues. We were sent here to find more of us, but all we've been doing is rescuing normal humans! This whole thing has been a waste of time!"

Reuben sighed, and his shoulders sagged. His face turned sorrowful. "Darius, listen. I'm sorry. I know this whole thing has been fruitless, but look."

He held the candle up to Calum once more, and Darius's eyes widened as the light turned green.

He stuttered for a moment, his eyes wide, and Reuben grinned.

"Nature magic?" Darius almost whispered, seemingly in awe.

Reuben continued to grin a knowing grin. "Yup."

Darius's eyes flicked between Calum and Reuben. "But there hasn't been . . ."

"I know." Reuben smiled, pulling the candle away.

Then, Darius walked across the room, coming to stand in front of Calum with earnest eyes and determination. "What's your name?"

He reached for her hand and took it, holding it between both his own gently.

I felt my grip tighten around her.

"Calum," she answered hesitantly.

"Well, Calum, we are going to get you out of here as soon as possible. Would you like that?" Darius questioned.

"I would like that very much," Calum answered softly, and I noticed that her lip trembled slightly. Tears were collecting on her eyelashes. My heart twisted, and for a moment, I thought she might break down. After everything that happened, I wouldn't be surprised.

"Are you really going to help us?" I questioned, not sure what to make of these two.

"Of course." Reuben stepped forward. "We will always help our own."

"What do you mean?" Calum asked before I got the chance.

"What Reuben means, Calum, is that we also have magic. We're just like you," Darius explained.

"Wait, but—how is that possible?" I stammered, looking from one to the other.

It felt crazy. One moment I thought Calum and her brother were the only ones with magic in the kingdom, and the next there were more. There were probably many more of them out there.

"It's this kingdom." Darius scoffed, grimacing. "It used to be common knowledge that there were a few with magic and that there was more to this world than the eye could see, but it only took a few generations to erase all of it. It's all just fairytales now."

"Well . . ." Calum hesitated, and I could see hope in her eyes. "How many are there? People with magic I mean?"

"Not as many as there used to be," Reuben responded, placing his hand on Darius's shoulder.

"Grab our things," he continued, speaking to Darius, who nodded and dropped Calum's hand.

I watched as Darius grabbed their bags and threw things into them, then turned to Reuben. "How are you going to get us out of here?"

Reuben grinned once more. "With magic, of course."

It only took a few more moments for them to be ready to leave. It was as if they had been expecting to make a quick departure, and it made me realize that these two were in just as much danger in the kingdom as we were. And that revelation made me think of the General. He was probably the one who had hunted down all those with magic. It made me shiver inwardly, and thinking back to the dungeon, I realized he was probably waking up. He was going to come after us, and those two were our only hope. We needed to get out of there as soon as possible.

"Ready?" Reuben asked, bringing me from my thoughts.

"Yes," I answered, the same time as Calum.

"Good," Darius responded and stepped forward, closing his eyes.

A moment passed, then another, and I swore a soft breeze caressed my cheek, but it was impossible in that room with no windows.

"There," Darius spoke, opening his eyes.

"Perfect," Reuben answered, looking at us.

In confusion, I looked down, and instead of seeing Calum and myself, I saw two totally different people. We didn't look like ourselves anymore. We wore fine clothes with intricate embroidery and looking up at Calum's face, I wasn't seeing Calum anymore. Instead, I saw a fine young woman in her late twenties with porcelain skin and dark eyes.

Her eyes widened as she looked into my face as well, and I knew that I didn't look like Adric anymore.

"That's amazing." Calum's voice rose in excitement, and I was pleased to hear that it was still her voice.

"It's a touch of air magic. I warped the light and air around you to look like that. It's just a disguise. You will still feel and sound the same." Darius smiled at Calum's excitement.

"You have air magic?" she questioned, and he nodded in response.

"What about you?" she turned to Reuben.

"Fire," he answered, and her smile faded.

Sorrow filled her eyes once more as she looked at him. I reached down and squeezed her hand in response.

A knock came from the door behind us, making me jump.

"Soldiers," Darius whispered, and we took several steps back from the door, panicked.

"Act casual," Reuben answered. Then, he commanded Darius, "Open it."

The door unlocked with a click.

Reuben swung the door open in a fluid motion and scoffed. "It's a little late, you know."

"My apologies," the soldier answered, and his eyes roamed around the room, landing on each of us.

"You didn't happen to see two individuals running around here, did you? They'd be dirty, a boy and a girl."

"No," Reuben answered firmly, letting annoyance enter his tone.

"My apologies, have a good night." The soldier bowed slightly, then disappeared down the hallway.

Reuben turned back to us, a frown on his face. "We need to go."

We nodded, and Reuben handed his bag to Darius.

"Follow us, but stay a few paces behind. No one will suspect anything," he instructed us.

I gripped Calum's hand in mine, telling myself we could do it.

Taking a deep breath, we followed them out into the hallway. All was quiet, and we paused to let the two of them get slightly ahead. Darius followed Reuben like an obedient servant, laden with their packs. I took Calum's hand and rested it on my arm as I had seen other older couples do.

It was difficult walking at a leisurely pace. All I wanted to do was run and get out of there as quickly as possible. I wanted to feel the fresh air in my lungs, but I managed to restrain myself.

We only passed two other soldiers, and I tried to act as casually as possible. My heart pounded so loud in my chest I thought it might give us away, but they only gave us a swift bow and continued on.

Turning down the next hallway, I saw a doorway, and relief coursed through me, but once we entered the room, I felt Calum's hand grip my arm, hard.

We were in the throne room again, heading toward the front entrance. Guards were stationed at every pillar, but after a quick glance, they gave us no mind.

It felt like we were going at the speed of a snail. The rainbow lights of the stained glass did not feel warm and beautiful then. They felt sinister with their jagged edges.

I took in deep, slow breaths. Almost there.

The door loomed before us, and as we approached, they opened. Fresh night air caressed my face, and the sounds of crickets met my ears.

Then, we were out, walking down the multitude of steps toward the front gate.

The stars shone overhead, and Calum's grip on me loosened, relaxed.

We were out.

Chapter 23

We made it out the front gates and out into the city easily. Once we were out of sight of the castle, Darius turned back and gave us a grin, and they both stopped to wait for us to catch up. As we drew closer, I noticed a bead of sweat sliding down his brow. The magic had to be taking a lot out of him. He tried his best not to show it.

"That was easy," he remarked, still smiling.

"No one let your guard down yet," Reuben answered, placing his hand on Darius's arm. "We need to find the stables."

That time, he spoke to Calum, but she just looked back at him dumbfounded. "I . . . I'm sorry. I don't know where they are," she stammered, looking between the two of them.

"You have the power of nature, don't you?" Darius asked, eyebrows raised.

"Well, yes. But I know how to do very little. I had very little training." She blushed, embarrassed.

Both of their eyes widened and Reuben spoke. "Apologies, Calum. We were being presumptuous. I'll help you."

He took her hand in his.

"Close your eyes," he instructed, and she did as she was told.

"Now reach out with your mind. Open your senses. Listen to the crickets, the living things around you."

Reuben watched her face, and her brow furrowed in concentration.

"Now focus on those living things. Reach out to them."

A moment passed and she murmured. "I think I feel them?" Her tone came out more as a question than a definite response.

"Good, search around. Feel the different—"

"I know where they are!" Calum's eyes flew open, and she looked at Reuben in astonishment.

Reuben's eyes widened as well, and then he grinned. "You're a fast learner."

"I felt everything! The humans were much harder, but the animals were right there, like they held a stronger presence."

"Humans aren't as in tune with nature as they once were," Reuben answered. "Interesting."

"Which way?" Darius interrupted.

Calum pointed down the road. "That way."

"Then let's go," Reuben answered, and we headed down the road with Calum leading us.

It was strange to me, not having Calum by my side. I was used to leading her, holding her hand. But she led us, hurrying down one street, then another. She was coming into herself, becoming her own person, separate from me. And with some surprise, I realized it made me a little bit sad. It made me wonder if she would still stay with me now that she didn't need me. I wasn't sure, but ultimately it was her own choice. We had to get out of there first.

We headed down through the city, making our way farther and farther from the castle. As the wall surrounding the city rose before us, we arrived at the stable that sat at its base. The stables stretched for quite a way down the side of the wall, and when we entered, I saw the stalls stretch out on either side of us.

Stable hands roamed the area, and the smell of horse hit my nostrils. There were tons of horses there. The stalls went on and on from one building to the next. These had to all be owned by the people living in the city, and it amazed me how such wealth could turn into so many animals for traveling.

"Thank you, Calum." Reuben smiled. He then greeted the stable hand who rushed up to us. He handed over a piece of paper, and the stable hand led us down the aisle, stopping in front of a stall.

"These two are yours," the man motioned to two stalls, side by side.

"You wouldn't happen to have any animals for sale, would you?" Reuben questioned.

The man shook his head. "Demand is high, and there aren't enough to go around."

Reuben sighed. "Thank you, anyway."

The man left us quickly, back the way he had come.

Darius opened the stall door in front of him and smiled. "I love taxes."

I peeked in the stall to see a perfectly groomed horse with fresh hay at its feet. A saddle sat on its stand in the corner, perfectly buffed and smelling of polish.

You could tell that the city was prosperous, and I knew it to be true after seeing no slums when we had arrived. It was impressive. But I knew it wouldn't last long. Whatever the previous king and queen had built would surely not last with the General being king. He was too greedy for something like that, and he craved power too much.

Before Reuben and Darius could begin to saddle their horses, Calum shouted, "Adric!"

She began to run down the hallway of stalls.

"Calum!" I called after her in shock as I ran after her, but she didn't turn around.

Our disguises dropped as we got further from Darius. Luckily there was no one else around at that point in the evening.

I began to breathe hard, still exhausted and malnourished, but thankfully she stopped in front of one of the stalls. I came to stand beside her, still panting from the sudden exertion.

What met my eyes shocked me so severely it took me a moment for my brain to register that what I was seeing was indeed real.

There she stood. Pumpkin. And looking past her, a figure lay on the hay, a bottle mostly drained in his hand. He was passed out, snoring softly.

"Cassius!" Calum squealed, opening the stall door, and running to him.

She dropped to her knees in front of him and grabbed him, pulling him into a big hug.

"Uhhh," he moaned, dropping the bottle from his hand to reciprocate the hug.

I watched from the stall door as he slowly became more conscious. Reuben and Darius came at a more leisurely pace to stand beside me. They raised their eyebrows at the mess of the man they saw inside, and I grinned, finding their reactions amusing.

"This is Cassius. He helped us escape the witch hunt and traveled with us here. We got separated before we got to the city, though," I tried to explain.

"I see," Reuben answered.

"Calum?" Cassius groaned, pulling away enough to look at her face through squinted eyes.

"What happened to you?" he continued, wrinkling his nose at her appearance and the smell.

She continued to smile, but it lessened somewhat. "It's a long story. It's just so good to see you. Are the others okay?" Her eyes searched his.

"They're fine. I believe they're still searching for the two of you. We split up," he answered, sitting up straighter.

He looked over her shoulder to see me and then the two beside me.

"Who are they?" He eyed them warily.

"This is Reuben and Darius. They're helping us escape," I said.

His features wrinkled in concern. "Escape? What are you escaping from?"

"The King," Calum answered, sad again.

He raised his eyebrows in surprise. "I see we've stepped up from the small village witch hunt."

I smiled. "Just a little bit."

Reuben shifted beside me. "We need to get going. Is he coming?"

"I am definitely coming," Cassius answered for himself, groaning as he braced himself against the wall to stand.

"Well, you better not slow us down," Darius replied, eyeing him warily.

"He won't," I answered.

The two left to finish saddling their horses, and I helped Cassius with Pumpkin.

"We have to hurry," I remarked, thinking about how long it had taken just to get us there.

Escaping the dungeon, getting lost in the castle, and finally leaving had taken several hours. If the city wasn't swarmed with soldiers by then, it surely would be soon.

When we finished, Cassius hefted Calum up into the saddle and grabbed the reins. He left his bottle forgotten in the hay.

"If we need to hurry, then we need more horses," Cassius spoke, glancing down the stalls one way then the other.

"Reuben already asked. There aren't any for sale," I answered.

Looking around once more, Cassius smiled a devious smile and reached for the next stall. A starling mare stood there, and he grabbed her halter.

"What are you doing?" I whispered in panic.

"Borrowing," he whispered back with a grin.

"You can't do that!" I yell-whispered.

"I already said, if we want to move fast, we need horses," he answered and grabbed the horse's saddle.

"Grab that one." He pointed to the stall next to his.

I debated for only a moment then opened the stall, my heart racing. I couldn't believe I was doing that. I had never stolen anything in my life. But Cassius was right. We had to get out of there fast.

I saddled the horse as quickly as I could, and we walked fast down the stalls to where Reuben and Darius waited.

Reuben smirked. "Good thinking."

Darius huffed out a laugh.

Then, we all mounted, and before heading out, Darius disguised us once more. With a final deep breath, we trotted out into the street and toward the front gate.

Chapter 24

The General groaned on the floor and peeled his eyes open. His head was pounding painfully, and it took him a moment to realize where he was.

He was alone. The torches still burned, but they were low. He was cold and stiff from lying on the stones, and he took his time sitting up as the blood rushed to his head.

The last thing he remembered was Lucian. He had stabbed Lucian directly in the chest. He had to be dead, but looking around, he didn't see a body. Had he survived? It was impossible. Perhaps the girl had healed him. There was no way of knowing.

Where were the guards? They had been there with him. Then as he thought, he remembered they had run away. At the first sight of danger, they had run. They could have stopped it all from happening. Because of their cowardice, the boy and girl had gotten away.

Anger seethed through him, and he stumbled to his feet. He moved slowly through the next room, and it was also empty where guards should have been. Everyone was missing and the air was filled with absolute silence.

He made it to the stairs and pulled himself up using the railing. When he opened the door at the top, there continued to be complete silence. Looking out the window, he could see that the very first streaks of dawn had turned the sky a light gray. Everyone was still sleeping soundly in their beds.

"My King!" A soldier rushed down the hall to meet him.

The General turned, anger seething in rolling waves inside of him. He spoke through gritted teeth. "Where is everyone?"

The soldier looked at him confused, stopping to stand in front of him. His eyes tracked over the General, noticing his rumpled clothes.

"What do you mean?" the soldier asked.

The General huffed out a sigh. "I was unconscious in the dungeon all night while the witch and her friend escaped. You're telling me that no one even noticed?"

The soldier's eyes widened, and he stumbled over his words. "Well, I mean, we were told to keep an eye out for a girl and boy who might have escaped. We've seen absolutely nothing, and we always have guards at the castle doors, so I'm sure they're here somewhere."

The General's eyes narrowed. He thought the two soldiers who had run were probably trying to cover themselves in case he found them. They had done the bare minimum, but at least they had done something.

The soldier continued to babble. "Well, now that I know, I'll relay the information and we'll increase the search."

"We need to search the city as well and inform the guards at the city gates. They could be anywhere. Remember that she has magic. They could have gotten out of the castle another way."

"Yes, General." The soldier nodded, but instead of running off, he hesitated.

"Yes?" the General questioned, raising his eyebrows.

"Well, I actually came to find you for something else."

"What is it?" The General was becoming impatient.

"The treasurer sent me. He says the chest that was brought several days ago is empty. He just opened it today to count it . . ."

The General was already gone, stalking down the hall in long strides. The soldier ran to keep up, and when they reached the treasurer, the General threw the door open with a loud bang, making the man behind the desk jump.

"My King!" The old man rose and bowed, his spectacles almost falling off his nose.

"Where is it?"

The frail man pointed, and the General recognized the chest immediately. It was the small chest that Reuben and his servant had brought from his successful mines. It was the chest filled with the most vibrant gems.

New anger filled him. It had all been a trick, a lie.

THE THINGS OF NATURE

He swiftly turned to the soldier again. "This chest was brought by Reuben and his servant. They are the ones I let stay here at the castle. Get some more soldiers and meet me there in their rooms."

The General turned to leave, but the soldier's timid voice rose once more. "General! Actually, they left in the middle of the night last night with a lord and lady."

The General turned slowly, eyes widening. "A lord and a lady?"

"Yes, sir."

"You realize there was no one else staying at the castle, right?"

"Um, no, sir."

The General pointed at the soldier, his eyes on fire with frustration. "You make sure that the city is searched completely. Look down every street and behind every bush. I want them found. Also, tell the royal infantry to prepare to leave. I suspect that they have already left the city."

"Yes, My King." The soldier bowed, then scurried off.

The General followed. He needed to prepare because he now understood what he was up against. Reuben had left in the night and upon their departure, the jewels had vanished. It was magic, plain and simple. It was clear that they had also found each other and were running together. Whatever they were planning, the General needed to hurry. It wasn't looking good. They had slipped right through his fingers.

He took his time cleaning up. The infantry would take the rest of the morning preparing with horses and rations.

They would leave as soon as the sun was high in the sky, but before that happened, the General needed something. He needed a better weapon. One that couldn't melt or be affected by magic.

He headed toward the royal barracks and entered the royal blacksmith's workspace. Weapons new and old covered every surface, as well as blueprints and letters. The place was a mess, covered in soot. None of that deterred the General.

"I need a weapon."

The blacksmith looked up startled. "My King!"

"I need a weapon that will not be affected by magic," he continued without pause.

The blacksmith took a moment, trying to understand the General's request.

"Um, I'm really sorry, sir, but we have nothing like that. I can show you some of our newest swords or daggers?" He reached toward a table laden with unused, sharp swords.

"No, no." The General looked around the room, and his eyes landed on a sword mounted to the wall. It caught his eye and held it.

The sword was different. It was almost like it was calling to him. It was strewn with cobwebs and dust, but the blade still glinted underneath, untarnished with rust. The steel of the blade was midnight black while the hilt was silver.

The General pointed. "What about that one?"

"Where? That?"

"Yes, that," the General retorted.

"Oh, I'm sorry, sir. That sword is not to be used."

"Why not?"

"Well, I'm not entirely sure, sir. The knowledge has been passed down. I'm sure it should not be used under any circumstances."

The General scoffed, strode forward, and grabbed the hilt. He easily lifted it from its stand and blew the dust off the blade. It gleamed in the faint light, and it almost hummed in his hands with life. That was a sword that held great strength. It was a sword he could most definitely use against a person with magic.

CHAPTER 25

Dawn arrived as we crossed the plains of grain outside the castle gates. We entered one of the towns surrounding the royal city and met only farmers and others busying themselves with their morning chores. The sun rose bright and by the time we reached the farther outskirts of the village, it was high in the sky.

We kept the horses moving at a fast pace, sometimes galloping, sometimes slowing to a trot to give them breaks. But the animals were strong and well rested. They kept up the pace until we finally came to a stop to water them at the edge of a wood.

I knew the Dark Forest would be looming before us at the end of the day. As long as we kept up the pace, we would reach it.

I also knew that the General would be coming after us. There was little to no chance he would let us go, especially after we had humiliated him the way we did. We had left him crumpled on the floor and had escaped the castle with no issues.

As we stood beside our horses, a mighty gust of wind zipped through, whipping my clothes and hair. Calum let out a soft screech as it whipped her skirts and yanked her.

"Sorry," Darius spoke and smiled. "I wanted to check to see if they were following us yet."

"You can do that?" I asked bewildered.

"Sure," he responded. "The wind can be a powerful force. With it, I can pick up shapes and outlines and even noises. With a powerful enough wind, I can hear things that happen a mile away."

"Do you eavesdrop much?" Cassius asked, a playful smile on his face.

"Only if it's necessary. I use it normally to gain intelligence."

"Darius," Reuben spoke his name in warning.

He rolled his eyes. "What? I didn't tell them anything."

I cautiously eyed the two of them. "What aren't you allowed to tell us?" I questioned.

Reuben turned to me with a sigh. "Only things pertaining to where we are from or our mission. We've already told you why we are helping you, but that is just one of our reasons. We disagree with the kingdom and its actions when it comes to killing people, but there is more to it than that. The fewer people who know the details of who we are or what we do, the safer we are."

"Just in case someone gets captured and interrogated," Darius added.

I thought for a moment then remembered something he had said earlier. "Back in the castle, you mentioned someone had sent you on this mission to rescue those with magic. Is that what you're talking about?"

Reuben sighed. "That is exactly what I'm talking about. You already know too much."

"Since we already know too much," Cassius cut in, "can you tell us at least which direction we are traveling in? Are we going south or north?"

"We continue west," Reuben answered.

"West?" I asked.

There was nothing to the west. The only thing in that direction was the Dark Forest and the villages that lined the base of the mountains after that. The mountains were impossible to pass and thinking about them reminded me of that fateful day when I had found Calum freezing slowly on one of the foothills. West was the direction we had been running from our entire journey. We were going back exactly the way we had come.

"Yes, west," Reuben answered. "That's all I will tell you."

He mounted his horse again and Darius followed.

Turning to Darius, Reuben asked, "Did you detect anything?"

Darius shook his head. "As far as I can tell, nothing has left the city gates yet."

"We are in luck then. We have a head start." Reuben smiled, and we headed off once more.

THE THINGS OF NATURE

We continued through farmland and forest and only stopped by some houses to grab Calum and me some new clothes since the ones we had from the dungeon were destroyed.

Reuben had gone into a small store and paid for the items, so at least I didn't have to feel bad about stealing again.

We took a moment to wash in a nearby stream, and then we were off again, and I felt infinitely better.

When evening came, the Dark Forest loomed in the distance. I tried to spot the wanderers' camp entrance, but it was so well hidden I missed it. I suppose you had to know exactly where it was to find it.

I felt sad then. That had been the last place we had seen our friends from the Dark Forest, and we were heading in the exact opposite direction of where they were looking for us. I felt a pang in my chest as I realized that we had forgotten to look for them on the road, but there was nothing we could do about it now. I was focused on getting away and that was what we were doing.

As we came to the edge of the forest, Reuben pulled us all to a stop, turning to Darius. "Are we too far away for your wind?"

Darius nodded and grinned. "Definitely too far."

"My turn then." Reuben jumped off his horse.

I was momentarily envious of his agility. I was completely stiff from the long ride and beginning to lose feeling in my legs and my seat, and my muscles felt like jelly.

I blinked in confusion as Reuben got down on his hands and knees and pressed his ear to the road. He looked absolutely ridiculous with his butt sticking up in the air, and he closed his eyes in concentration.

"What is he doing?" Calum questioned Darius, looking at Reuben as if he had lost his mind.

"Shhhh," Darius answered, but then seeing as we were all about to ask another question, he amended, "he's listening to the center of the earth."

"Excuse me?" Cassius asked. "What was his power again?"

"Fire. Now be quiet or it will take longer." Darius looked forward into the distance and promptly ignored us.

And it did take several minutes that felt more like fifteen in the complete silence. Then Reuben rocked back on his heels, wiping the dirt from his face. He turned to us, his face downcast in concern.

"It doesn't look good."

"What doesn't look good?" I asked.

"They've left the city, and there are about fifty of them, all on horseback."

Cassius looked at him, not believing. "How exactly do you know that?"

Reuben turned to face him, annoyed at the pestering. "I have the power of fire, and there is no bigger fire than that of the center of the earth. Just below the earth's crust, the entire center is made of molten fire. Now, things on the surface make vibrations in the ground, and that transfers to the fire where I can then feel it. It has taken me around a century to be able to perfect that particular skill. With more practice, I can more accurately tell what is occurring on the surface."

"A century?" Cassius questioned.

Reuben nodded. "I am a little older than I appear."

"Wait. How is that even possible?" I asked, aghast.

"I'm not sure how much you know about those with magic, but if it is used properly or in the way it was intended, then it can elongate your life. If you use your gift wrongly, on the other hand, your life will be long, but you will shrivel up to be only a glimpse of your former self."

And I did know that. The centaurs had told us as much after our encounter with the witch in the Dark Forest. I had forgotten after everything that had happened, but now I wondered if Calum continued to use her magic, would she remain as I saw her? Would I continue to age while she stayed young and beautiful?

"How old are you?" Cassius turned to Darius, eyeing him.

He answered with a smile. "Only thirty-five, but I stopped aging at twenty-eight."

I felt a sense of relief that he also wasn't a century old. It was unnerving.

"And don't worry," Darius continued. "Someone like Reuben is actually quite rare."

"Well, that's good to hear," Cassius shuttered.

Darius smiled. "You'll get used to it."

Reuben rolled his eyes, grabbing the reins to his own horse and Calum's. "Alright, everyone. We should be able to rest a few hours before we continue on. I'll keep watch."

He led us off the road down the line of trees. To the right were normal woods, but to the left were the old trees of the Dark Forest. It was like we were walking the line between the modern world and a much more ancient one.

We stopped once the road became invisible, and I slowly dismounted. My thighs trembled, and my muscles screamed in protest. Without unpacking anything, I let myself fall to the ground, relishing the stillness of the earth.

Calum joined me to one side and then Cassius on the other.

The stars twinkled to life overhead as the sky fully darkened into night. We only had a few hours to rest before we continued to move. I needed to ask Cassius something. It gnawed at me.

"Cassius?"

"Hmm?" he mumbled.

"The others, did they make it out of the wanderers' camp safely?"

He cracked his eyes open and looked over to where Calum and I waited for his response.

"They're fine. In fact, they were completely unharmed. Sterling kind of snapped, you see. I think he had a lot of pent-up anger inside of him, and it exploded. The soldiers had no chance."

"So, they're dead? The soldiers?" Calum asked meekly.

"They are. All of them." He paused, then decided it best to continue. "It was necessary. They would have followed you if we hadn't taken care of them."

"Do you know where they are, Sterling and the others?" I asked again, but I remembered what he had said before.

"I have no clue," he answered. "Hopefully they will follow us. That many soldiers leaving the city was probably quite a spectacle. They might ask around and realize who they're after."

With that, he rolled over and ended the conversation, but I felt a little bit of hope. Maybe the others would find us after all. It was a slim chance, but I dearly hoped they would.

Chapter 26

"Wake up." Reuben's voice met my ears.

When I opened my eyes, there was only darkness and the light of the moon and stars. It felt like I had just closed my eyes, and I let out a groan as I moved my aching limbs. Calum sat up beside me, just as groggy and confused.

"You've rested long enough, it's time to go." Reuben helped us to our feet, and my body protested every movement.

We clambered onto our horses, and we moved forward in silence. The world around us was awake with the incessant sound of crickets and the hoot of distant owls, but it felt like I was traveling in a fog. The only one who seemed unfazed was Reuben. He hadn't slept, and he appeared perfectly fine.

THE THINGS OF NATURE

We moved at a slow pace and took the night winding through the Dark Forest. It felt less menacing then as I knew that the witch was gone. The woods were safe once more.

As the sky began to lighten, food was passed out, and we quickly fed our hungry stomachs. We stopped for only a few moments after that to water the horses, and then we continued.

"Calum, may I ask you a question?" Reuben slowed his horse to come beside hers.

"Of course," she answered.

"I know this might be a sensitive subject, but when you were down in that dungeon, I swear I felt fire. Not just any fire, of course, but made fire. Was there a fire wielder down there with you?"

"There was." She swallowed and turned her eyes to look ahead at the road and away from him.

"I apologize for asking. When I felt it, it woke me. I didn't feel it again after that and then you arrived . . ."

She cut him off. "It was my brother."

Reuben raised his eyebrows.

"And he's gone." She still didn't look at him.

"I'm sorry," Reuben responded softly, and I could tell that he truly was.

Her eyes flicked to him. "It's alright. I hadn't seen him since I was quite young."

There were several moments of silence, then Reuben continued, "You know, earth, fire, air, and water, the four elements, are the most common gifts of magic. Most who end up possessing a gift end up with one of those four, just like Darius and myself."

"Wait, then, what about me?" Her eyes, filled with unshed tears, now eyed Reuben, distracted.

"You're special, Calum. That was why Darius was so surprised to see that candle turn green. I just wanted you to know that."

He gave her a soft smile then kicked his horse forward so that he was in the front once more.

The day continued to brighten, and by the time the sun was overhead, we could see the end of the Dark Forest. We were almost home, and it made my heart race at the idea of seeing the village again.

"Time to stop," Reuben announced as we neared the edge. He jumped off his horse and again pressed his ear to the dirt.

We waited several moments before Cassius interrupted. "Anything?"

"Shhh." Darius looked at him accusingly.

"This doesn't make sense," Reuben answered, surprising us.

"What doesn't make sense?" Darius asked, eyebrows furrowed.

"Hold on. Let me listen again."

Silence reigned again, but that time it only took Reuben a few moments before he jumped to his feet.

"They've already entered the Dark Forest. In fact, they're only about a twelve-hour march away."

"Wait, what?" Darius looked down at Reuben in shock. "With fifty soldiers they should be moving slower than us, not faster."

"Well," Cassius cut in, "if they were at full gallop the entire time, then it's possible."

"You know that's not possible," Darius replied.

"Maybe you're reading it wrong?" I questioned Reuben, but he shook his head.

"No, I'm not wrong. It's just odd. It's as if something was helping them along, like magic. But we know they aren't using magic."

"Either way, we need to get moving," Darius replied.

"You're right." Reuben swung back into the saddle. "Let's go."

⋄⇾≡◉⇽⋄

The General felt amazing. The sound of thundering hooves filled his core, and he felt that strength inside of him. He felt invincible.

A wind pushed them from behind, and the ground seemed to jump to meet their feet. None of the soldiers or horses broke a sweat as they flew down the road, making incredible time. The sword at his hip still hummed in satisfaction.

They hadn't stopped during the night or even during the following day. No one ever needed to. The whole thing was definitely suspicious. There had to be some kind of magic at work, or maybe it was a coincidence, but the General chose to ignore those feelings. He felt too good, and besides, it was all in his favor.

The General turned to the second in command beside him. "Soldier!"

The soldier turned. "Yes, sir?"

"When we reach them, feel free to kill the others, but leave me the girl."

"Yes, My King." The soldier nodded and relayed the message.

The General continued to smile. She had slipped through his fingers too many times. With the new sword at his side, he would be able to kill her whether she had magic or not.

⇌

We were out of the Dark Forest and nearing the village. Traveling through the first time had felt like such a long journey, but we were moving as quickly as we could, trees and rocks swirling past us.

I recognized the small bridge as we neared it. Following the little stream going under it would lead us to a little abandoned cabin in the woods. It was the place that Cassius had first brought us when we escaped the villagers. It seemed like a lifetime ago, almost surreal.

We had been different people back then, especially Calum. She had been timid, sad, and scared. But coming back, she was riding her own horse and magic filled her veins.

Then a sinking feeling came into my chest. I was practically the same. I was still in love with her like I had been then, and I was still too scared to tell her. She was becoming her own person. She soon wouldn't need me anymore, and there I was, still clinging to her in hope.

"Stop!" Darius yelled, and we pulled our horses to a stop in front of the bridge.

"What is it?" Reuben asked, swiveling his head around.

"I can feel them," Darius answered, eyes widening in amazement.

"How is that possible?" Reuben questioned. "That means they're only a few miles away."

His eyes darted down the road, back the way we had come.

Darius shrugged. "I know. I don't understand it. We've been moving as quickly as we can. Do you think we can still make it?"

"Make it where?" Cassius cut in.

"The mountains," Reuben answered.

I knew the woods there better than anyone else. I spoke up reluctantly. "There's no way. They'll reach us before we hit the village if they keep coming like this."

"What do we do?" Calum whispered, looking at Reuben in dismay.

"I . . . I don't know," he ran his fingers through his hair in frustration.

A heavy sense of helplessness blanketed us as we looked at each other, but then Cassius broke the silence. "I can hold them off," he murmured.

"What? No!" I turned to him.

There was no way we were going to leave anyone behind.

"I can hold them—distract them long enough for you guys to reach the village," he spoke stronger now, more determined.

"Do you realize what you're offering?" Reuben questioned quietly.

"I do," he answered.

His eyes were hard.

"Cassius, there must be another way," Calum begged, but he shook his head.

"There's no other way we can slow them down." Then he gave her a soft smile. "Don't worry, Calum. Just do me a favor and get to those mountains."

"Here. Take this." Reuben tossed a small pendant on a golden chain to him, and he caught it.

"What's this?" Cassius questioned him.

"A good luck charm . . . with magic," he answered.

"Well, thank you." Cassius nodded, slipping it into his pocket.

Then he turned his horse to face back the way we had come.

"Don't do this," Calum begged again.

Darius reached over and grabbed her reins. "We have to go."

Then we were moving again, the hooves of the horses clopping on the wood of the bridge. I felt for a split second that maybe I should stay, too. I could help Cassius hold them off. But I was no soldier. I had no skills with a blade. I would probably be a hindrance, and I knew deep down that I couldn't leave Calum. Even though I knew it, I still felt bad as I looked back the way we had come.

Cassius took in a deep breath and unsheathed his sword from where it rested at Pumpkin's side. He rested the sword on his lap and didn't look back, his eyes focused on the road in front of him.

CHAPTER 27

The General smiled as he glimpsed the mountain peaks in the distance. They had been informed by other travelers they had passed that the small group had been making their way toward those mountains. Fools. They would be pinned between the mountain range and his incoming soldiers. There was nowhere else to run.

Then the General glimpsed something in the distance. As they drew near, he saw that it was a young, blond man sitting on a horse, blocking their path. He looked relaxed, his sword on his lap.

The General slowed his horse, then came to a stop, the rest of the soldiers following.

"I suggest you remove yourself from the road so that we might pass," the General called out, a healthy distance away from the boy.

"I apologize, but I cannot," the boy returned, unfazed by the demand.

The General's eyebrows raised. "You *must* move. I am your king. Unless you want to be trampled by my army, I suggest you step aside."

The boy just lifted his chin in defiance. "I'm afraid you will have to either go through me or go back the way you came. Either way, this direction is not an option for you."

The General smiled in surprise. That young man was quite intriguing.

"May I ask why you are blocking the path?" he inquired.

"I have my reasons," the young man answered after taking a moment to figure out his answer.

"Perhaps you are trying to protect some friends?" the General asked.

The boy kept silent for a moment, his eyes searching the soldiers. "Perhaps," he finally relented.

The General drew his sword. "Well, I'm afraid your efforts are in vain. Whether you are protecting the witch or not, you will be moved. Or . . ." Instead of finishing his sentence, he turned to the soldier at his side. "Grab him. He could have information."

The soldier nodded and also drew his sword.

"Retrieve him, please," the General commanded, and five soldiers rode forward, swords raised.

The young man took in a deep breath and raised his own sword, eyeing the ones coming toward him. Then, surprising everyone, he kicked his horse forward. He galloped toward the incoming danger, and the soldiers returned the favor, kicking their own steeds into a gallop to meet him. When they met, blood sprayed. The young man pulled his horse, first one way, then the next, his sword singing as they danced through the soldiers. A soldier swung, but he dodged, leaning backward in his saddle so the steel just grazed his nose, and in the next instant, his sword flung out, catching the soldier in the back. The young man knew how to fight.

"You, go!" The General motioned to more soldiers, and they moved forward.

Cassius killed or injured at least five soldiers before they had him properly surrounded. He was perfectly unharmed, and he turned his horse in a full circle, but there were only the tips of swords each way he turned.

"Drop the sword!" The General moved forward, and the young man only eyed him for a moment before letting his sword fall out of his hands and to the dirt.

Soldiers dismounted and grabbed him, pulling him off his horse. It was all over as quickly as it had started.

The General frowned at the bodies in the road and glared at the young man. "Tie him up. This boy is no peasant. We need answers."

More soldiers dismounted as they realized that they were stopping. If the General wanted to interrogate him, it would probably take some time, but they certainly had time. Time was in their favor. The runaways wouldn't get far with the mountains blocking their path anyway.

The General thought about that as they tied the young man to a tree on the side of the road. His eyes pierced into him, trying to see the answers he desired through his skin, but the young man glared back, not afraid of the General in the least.

"No mere peasant could have pulled off what you just did," the General began, but the boy didn't respond.

He didn't even blink. He simply looked bored and in no rush whatsoever.

"Where were you trained?" the General questioned.

Again, there was no answer.

The General felt the eyes of all the soldiers around him, pressuring him to get answers and perform like a true general. He pulled out his golden sword and pointed it at the young man.

"Answer me," he commanded, and when the silence continued, the General sliced his upper arm, garnering a hiss of pain out of him.

The General raised his sword again. The young man answered, "I was trained in Amartoth. I am a soldier like the rest of you." His eyes were pained, but he managed to look at the soldiers surrounding him.

The General blinked, surprised at his answer, and turned to the soldiers. "Do any of you recognize him?"

He didn't, maybe the others did. There was no response from the surrounding soldiers. He turned back to the boy. "You're lying."

The General assumed that must be the case and stepped forward to nick him again with his sword, but a soldier stopped him, placing a hand on his arm.

"Apologies, My King, if I may, I would like to interrogate this man." The soldier spoke strongly and without fear. "I am quite good at getting answers out of those who are not so willing." He smiled.

The General nodded in approval.

If the soldier wanted to take a go at the boy, then he wouldn't deny him. There was a fire in his eyes that the General recognized, so the General stepped back, letting the soldier take over.

"The name is Adam." The soldier stepped forward.

He had light brown hair, cut short, and piercing blue eyes. His eyes studied Cassius, sizing him up, and then he stepped forward, drawing his dagger from his hip. He flipped the blade deftly in his hand and took another step forward so his boots were almost touching Cassius's.

"And you killed my brother," he whispered just loud enough for Cassius to hear him and no one else.

Cassius's eyes widened in surprise, then softened. "I'm sorry."

Adam sneered.

Cassius could see it now. The soldier was older than the others. He had more years in which he had gained confidence and rank. He had dared to step forward and confront Cassius himself. It was an act of revenge, plain and simple. Whether he got answers or not, it didn't really matter to him.

Adam leaned forward once more and smiled. "I know who you are, deserter."

He was the closest in age to Cassius compared to the newer recruits, so it made sense that he would recognize him.

He took a step back, satisfaction gleaming in his eyes, but all he got was a smile. If he had intended to scare Cassius, it hadn't worked.

He frowned and raised his blade to point at his chest. He began his questioning. "Were you with the witch?"

Cassius didn't answer, but Adam had expected that.

"Answer. This is your final warning." Adam let the silence hang in the air for a few moments more, but all Cassius did was smile to himself.

The only thing on Cassius's mind was that his friends were that much closer to the mountains. All he had to do was hold out a little while longer, and so far, he had held them much longer than he had expected. He had assumed the army would cut right through him, so it was more than he had hoped for. He was giving Calum time and that was all he cared about.

Adam backhanded him, making his face sting and his lip split.

"Where are they heading?" Adam grabbed Cassius before he could fall to the side.

Cassius looked at him once more, saying nothing.

"If you aren't going to talk, then this is going to get ugly, fast." Adam seethed quietly in warning, but Cassius just gave a half-smile in return.

Adam's free fist connected with Cassius's stomach, making Cassius gasp and bend over as he tried to catch his breath.

"Where are they going?" he repeated. "There are only mountains to the west."

Once Cassius was able to breathe again, he straightened himself up and locked eyes with the soldier. Then he smiled, a genuine, big smile. Adam eyed him warily, unsure of himself. Looking around, he saw the confusion on the other soldiers' faces and concluded that Cassius was mocking him.

"Well?" Adam raised his eyebrows.

Cassius just smiled.

Adam grimaced. "This is your own fault."

He brought his knife down on Cassius's thigh and Cassius cried out in pain. Adam ripped the knife free and blood began to flow, but not too fast. He hadn't hit the artery.

"Soldier!" the General called out a warning, stepping forward.

Adam turned. "We've tried being nice, and it's not working. We need him to know that we are serious, and we are serious about getting answers."

He turned back to Cassius. "Ready to talk?"

Cassius smiled, a weaker smile, but it was still there, which enraged Adam even further.

"Talk!" Adam commanded, his cheeks becoming flushed with anger, and when no response came, he slashed

Cassius across the chest, cutting his clothing and into his skin. It was only a surface wound, but it bled all the same.

"Talk!" Adam continued to shout, and he took out his rage on Cassius with his fists.

Between each hit, all Cassius could think about was time. He was giving his friends time, as much time as he possibly could.

That was why he smiled. He appeared to be losing, but in the end, he was accomplishing his goal.

The world slowed with pain, and Cassius ended up sliding down the bark of the tree. He came to rest on the forest floor, his head hanging forward, barely conscious.

"That's enough, soldier." The General stepped forward, finally ending Adam's tirade.

The General grimaced at Cassius as blood dripped from his lips and spread across his clothing. His face swelled and his eyes were closed. There was no more smiling, and even if they tried, there would be no more answers out of him.

They had failed. Cassius had won.

The General turned to go. "Time to leave. We know where they're headed."

Another soldier stepped forward. "What do we do with him?"

"Leave him," Adam replied. "Just like he left us, we will leave him."

The soldiers looked at him in confusion, not knowing who Cassius was or that he was a deserter, but they did as Adam said. They saw with their own eyes what he had done to Cassius, and no one was going to get in his way.

As the soldiers left, one by one, Cassius sat with his pain. He tried to focus his mind on other things, but the pain always made him lose focus and drew him back in.

Once the final soldier was out of sight, and the pounding of hooves had faded, he finally looked up. He was alone, and thankfully, he hadn't been severely harmed. Every blow had lacked an edge. Every hit had just missed something or landed not as hard as it could have.

He squeezed the medallion in his pocket. He had held it the entire time, never letting go. Perhaps it was lucky after all.

Then, a noise caught his attention, and through the underbrush came three figures. One was large with silver hair, the next tall and lean with brown hair and a big smile, and the last of stocky build with leadership in his eyes.

Cassius smiled once more, even through the pain.

If he was seeing what he thought he was seeing, then luck was definitely on his side.

Chapter 28

We made it to town, and to not look too suspicious, we slowed our horses. Spring was in full bloom and people were out and about. Even though the place was so familiar, it felt smaller. Everyone we passed stared; they were not used to too many outsiders, and funny enough, there was no indication of anyone recognizing me. It was weird to think I had changed so much in such a short time. Sure, I was dressed differently and on an elegant horse, but I was sure I looked the same, even if I didn't feel the same.

As we exited the village, we nudged our horses forward again, and soon we passed by the small path that led to where our cabin had been. Looking through the trees, I saw nothing, like the building had never even been there. If we followed it, we would probably only have found some charred remains to remind us that something had been there at all.

The sun sank below the horizon, and soon it was dark. Clouds covered the moon and stars, making it impossible to see in the pitch-black. Before, the light of the moon and a road had guided us, but now there was nothing except wilderness and the rolling hills that made the foothills of the mountains. When our horses began to trip, we finally stopped, unable to go farther.

"We should keep going on foot," Darius remarked, jumping from his horse.

"Can we?" I questioned, only seeing impenetrable darkness and shadows.

"No," Reuben responded. "This undergrowth is too dense. We need to at least wait for the clouds to disperse. We have traveled far enough from any roads or people that we should be safe."

"Can you do something?" I asked Darius.

His eyes widened in disbelief.

"Move the clouds?" he questioned.

I tried to explain. "With your wind thing."

He grinned and laughed. "Definitely not. Even if I could, I'd be completely drained."

I turned away in embarrassment. I certainly didn't know the limits of magic. I barely knew what Calum was capable of—not that we had had much time to discuss it.

"So, what do we do now?" Calum asked.

Reuben pulled his bags off his horse. "Rest. And we won't be needing the horses anymore. They won't make it through this kind of growth or the hills."

We followed his example, and with a nudge, we sent the horses back the way we had come.

We settled down onto the packed earth, all of us completely exhausted and drained.

The silence was stunning compared to the pounding of hooves that we had been so used to for the past several days. The quiet was calming, and the darkness beckoned us into sleep.

Only a few moments passed before Calum's voice rose in a whisper beside me. "Adric?"

"Hmm?"

"I don't want to die."

I opened my eyes in shock and tried to see her through the darkness. "We aren't going to die. We're almost to the mountains."

"I know . . . but it's still possible we won't make it, and I guess what I'm trying to say is, that I feel like my life has finally started. Before we were run out of the village, I was living in this fog. I was unhappy. I'm sorry, Adric. It wasn't you, it was just our situation. Since leaving, I feel like I've woken up. I feel alive and free. I don't want to run away anymore. I want to live."

I was surprised to hear her say those words, but I understood. This journey had made her realize so many things. She had magic. She wasn't helpless. She had found confidence. We had made friends and seen so much. Her world had been turned upside down, but because of that, she had found purpose.

It made me think back to when I had first found her, lost in the woods. That was the turning point in my life and when I felt my life had begun. I almost felt sad realizing that she didn't feel the same. But she had found it now. She had a reason to live, just like I had found my reason back then.

I took her hand and squeezed it. "Don't worry, Calum. You have the three of us here, and we won't let you die."

※

We were leaped upon as we slept. Noise immediately filled the quiet night with the shout of commands as a man yanked me to my knees. My wrists were tied hastily with rope, and they burned as I tried to twist my hands out. Torches rose up to illuminate the night, and I saw the others were in the same predicament I was. They lined us up in a row, all on our knees with our hands bound behind our backs.

Kneeling like that felt all too familiar, and the helplessness I had felt in the castle washed over me again.

The General stepped forward, the shadows melting away as he came into the torchlight. He smiled and my heart sank. That was it. It was over.

"We meet again." The General grinned. "It was easy enough to find you. Almost like you wanted to be found."

We remained silent as he spoke. Glancing at the others, I saw they only had eyes for him. The fear was palpable, at least for me and Calum. I saw in Reuben's and Darius's eyes that they still thought they could get out of it somehow, like this couldn't be it. There had to be a way. But unless they somehow could defeat fifty soldiers with their magic, there was no getting out of it.

It made me wonder if they had ever been in predicaments like that before, but I didn't have much time to wonder. The General stepped forward, slowly unsheathing his sword from his waist.

There was something different about that sword. The blade was black, almost invisible in the night except for where the torches reflected off its surface. The hilt was old silver, flecked with discoloration and age.

The General held the blade up to his face as if to inspect it. "Amazing, isn't it?"

He slashed the blade through the air with a flick of his wrist, making my heart leap into my throat. The blade hummed with a sharp vibration as it cut the air.

"Where did you find that?" Reuben whispered.

I looked over at him in surprise to see that his face had gone pale in the torchlight.

He knew something. He had either seen the blade before, or he had heard about it.

I looked at the blade more closely, but I couldn't make out anything. I just prayed that he wouldn't use it on Calum or myself. I had no idea what it could do, and after having my eyes opened to all the magic surrounding us, and by the look on Reuben's face, I assumed it probably wasn't good.

The General didn't answer Reuben's question. "It's the perfect sword for a witch hunter. The blade cannot be broken or melted. I've tried. It's the perfect weapon against your kind."

"You don't know what you're talking about," Reuben retorted.

The guard holding him gave him a yank to silence him.

The General frowned and pointed the blade at him, the tip almost nicking his neck. Reuben didn't falter. His eyes bore into the General's, daring him to do it.

"I wasn't going to pick you to go first, but you're begging for it," the General said.

He liked being in that position of power. He liked playing with us, holding our lives in his hands.

Calum spoke up from beside me. "Please, don't."

I groaned internally as she got the General's attention.

I couldn't believe what she was doing. It was a repeat of what had gone down with Lucian, but now she was trying to protect our friends. She was being selfless, just like before. Once again, she was willing to give her life without hesitation.

"Calum!" I yelled out, frustrated and fearful.

I couldn't watch her die. I couldn't do it. I still loved her. I had followed her through the wilderness and the Central Kingdom. I had never left her side. I had done my best to protect her, even if it had mostly been the friends we had met along the way who had done the protecting. I had watched her grow and realize that she did have a purpose and that she wasn't useless or a burden. I had watched her blossom into her own person, and I couldn't watch that beautiful person be destroyed before my eyes.

"Witch." The General moved to stand before her. "There is no running away this time."

He raised the blade, and it continued to hum with anticipation. Calum's eyes were wide, but she didn't falter.

"Leave her alone!" I yelled at the General.

He looked over at me, amused.

"Your boyfriend is trying to protect you. How sweet," the General mocked. He didn't move his sword away from Calum's throat.

"Please, don't hurt her," I continued to beg, desperate.

It was the only thing I could do. I wasn't a strong soldier. I didn't have any magic. But I could beg, and I would do anything I could to stop that from happening, so I kept begging.

"Perhaps she has put a spell on you, boy. Perhaps when she is dead you will be free, and you will thank me."

The General trained his eyes back on Calum.

"No! Don't!" I screamed, and Reuben and Darius looked on with wide eyes and pale faces.

"Don't do it," Reuben added, his deeper voice cutting through. "You don't know what will happen if you do this."

The General merely rolled his eyes and lifted his sword, ready to swing.

I couldn't look away. I couldn't.

Calum squeezed her eyes shut in anticipation, and my heart burst with anger and agony at the whole situation.

The sword came down, and I gave one final yell of outrage. But before the blade met her skin, it disintegrated, turning to dust.

Silence reigned across the clearing and seconds ticked by, one second, then another. The dust twinkled, settling to the forest floor gently and silently.

Calum opened her eyes as she felt nothing, and her eyes landed on the silver hilt, still in the General's hand, but there was no more blade.

The General let the hilt fall from his fingers as he stood there in complete shock.

As the last remnants of the dust caressed the blades of grass on the forest floor, they exploded.

The General and his soldiers went flying with the force of the wind into the darkness. The four of us on our knees flew to our backs on the grass as the wind raked across our bodies. The loud crack of the explosion made my ears pop and ring, and soon after, I heard trees snapping and crashing all around us with the force of the gale, but none landed on us. They had all fallen away from us as if we were at the very center of where the wind had been released. All light winked out as the torches were all blown out, and we were left in utter darkness.

Shouts of pain and fear met my ears, and I found myself calling out as well for Calum, but my ears still rang and debris littered the forest floor, making it dangerous to move. Luckily, the force of the wind had mostly sailed over us.

As the ringing began to dissipate from my ears, I heard something else.

Several yards from my feet, I heard the sound of breathing. It was low, guttural, and definitely not human.

THE THINGS OF NATURE

The breathing was too loud, too low. It had to come from something big.

I froze in the darkness as fear filled me once more. Whatever it was, I didn't want it to know I was there.

I waited as I heard it take a deep breath, and then it screeched. I scrunched up my face in pain as I was unable to cover my ears. Whatever that thing was, it was huge, and it was very angry. The noise had to be heard for miles.

My heart raced in my chest, but now that the forest was flattened surrounding us, I could see the moon and stars shining overhead. Something glinted beside me—a sword.

I listened as the creature took one step, then another. It was moving away from me.

Determination filled me, and I slowly rolled so the blade of the sword was against the ropes tying my hands to my back. I began working vigorously, and in a few moments, my hands snapped free. Then, I grabbed the sword and brought it to my chest. I had a weapon. It made me feel infinitely better even though I had no idea what I was up against.

Calum.

I had to find her.

I reached out into the darkness, but there was only grass where she had previously been.

"Calum," I whispered. There was no reply.

I heard shouting across the new clearing and froze. I was beginning to be able to see the outline of the creature against the backdrop of the stars, and it was huge, standing at the height of a full-grown pine. It was not just its height, but also the massive size of its body which was the size of a multiroom building.

I reached out again, and that time, I crawled on my hands and knees, frantically searching. Several yards away my hand connected with something. Feeling it, I could tell it was hair, very curly hair.

"Calum," I whispered and took her into my arms, leaving the sword at my side.

Her body was limp, but when I shook her, she let out a soft moan. My chest filled with relief again.

We had to get out of there.

"Adric?" she whimpered.

"Yes, Calum, I'm here," I whispered back.

"I hit my head," she responded.

I slowly brought her to sit upright.

I unbound her hands, throwing the rope to the side. She reached up to touch her head.

"We need to get out of here."

"What happened?" she slurred.

She was still groggy and confused.

"There was an explosion, and there is some kind of monster. We need to go."

She looked around the clearing, and her eyes landed on its hulking form, a small way off.

She continued looking around. "Where're Reuben and Darius?"

She was becoming more lucid and awake.

My heart clenched at her words. I had been so busy trying to get Calum out that I hadn't given them a second thought.

"Over here," Reuben's voice rose from several yards away.

Calum began to get to her feet, and I was going to follow, but a voice rose from across the clearing. "No, you don't."

Chapter 29

The General stumbled out of the shadows toward us. He had his sword raised before him, but his clothes were torn, and there were scratches along his skin. He was torn up pretty badly, and I quickly realized that one of his arms hung limply by his side, probably broken.

His eyes were filled with fire, and he stumbled toward us.

I grabbed the sword beside me and held it out in warning, but that did nothing to deter him.

"You are going nowhere," the General hissed, but Calum continued to rise to her feet and face him. I stood beside her.

"Leave us alone," Calum spoke strongly, and there was no fear in her voice, only determination.

"Get back on your knees," the General barked out.

THE THINGS OF NATURE

"No," Calum answered, and the General tripped, catching himself. He tried to move forward again, but his foot was caught.

"Stop this!" he called out, but his boots were already crawling with grass and vines.

"You killed my brother." Calum's voice was steady. "And you were going to kill me."

"You're a witch!" the General exclaimed in frustration.

Calum took in a steadying breath, closing her eyes for a moment, and then let it out. Her eyes opened. "Yes. Yes, I am a witch."

I watched as her eyes began to glow green, soft at first, and then becoming bright like the stars. The grass swiftly clung and climbed its way up the General's legs. The General yelled out, dropping his sword. He began to rip at the thickening vines and grass but as quickly as he tore them away, they grew back. Soon he was forced to his knees as the greenery pulled him toward the earth. His muscles strained, but it was no use.

In shock, I stared at her, but she looked at the General, eyes steady.

"Calum, stop," I murmured, taking her hand in mine.

I couldn't believe she was doing that. She was actually going to kill him. I wanted the General dead just as much as she did, but I didn't want his death hanging over her head. She had always seen the good in people. She had always been gentle and kind. It was not like her to do something like that.

"Calum, stop," I repeated, and she finally looked at me, the grass pausing as well.

By then the General couldn't move. He was on his knees instead of us, and he grunted, anger still flashing in his eyes.

"Let me." The words were out of my mouth before I even realized what I was saying.

I could be the one to kill him. I could do it.

The entire journey I had watched Calum flourish into herself. I had done nothing. I was merely there, observing from the sidelines as everything occurred. I had been weak, unable to protect her like the others had. I had been unable to stop the General twice now. I had been unable to tell her how I felt about her.

I could change that. I could finally do something. I could finally *be* someone in her eyes, maybe.

Perhaps I could save her from that one thing.

I lifted the sword in my hand and stood taller. "Let me," I spoke with more conviction, determined.

"Okay," she whispered, her eyes still blossoming green.

I turned from her to the General and took the few steps to stand before him. His eyes held a hint of fear in them. He was just a normal man like any other. But he had done so much to us, so much.

I took in a shaky breath and took my eyes from his. I glanced at his chest only long enough to make sure I hit true, and then I turned away. Pulling my sword free, I turned my back on him, my eyes landing on Calum as she stared at me.

I couldn't look at him. I couldn't look at what I had done. Even though I knew it was necessary, the look in his eyes still burned in the back of my head, and I knew it would for a long time. But I had saved Calum that fate. She wouldn't have to live with the weight of death on her heart.

Her eyes faded, dimmed, then turned back to their normal dark shade.

"You did it," she whispered, almost in disbelief.

"I did," I answered.

Another shriek from the monster startled both of us out of our stupor, and I hurriedly grabbed her arm. I had to get her out of there, and hopefully the others, as well.

Looking around to find where the beast was, I saw it. Slinking toward us as if it were a giant cat, its belly brushing the earth, its eyes were directly upon us as it made its way. We must have made too much noise and drawn its attention.

I made to pull Calum and make a run for it, but she pulled back.

"Wait," she spoke.

"We need to go!" I practically shouted.

"She's happy," she said, only looking at the monster.

"I don't think it matters whether it's happy or not. I'm pretty sure it'll still eat us," I answered. I found it hard to believe she could really understand the monster, and I couldn't understand how she could possibly know it was happy.

Calum didn't budge as it drew closer, and all I could do was stand there and sweat.

I watched as it formed out of the darkness. It was black with spikes traveling down its spine and tail. It was incredibly well-fed, and we could have lived inside it comfortably if it were a house. Its four feet consisted of three front toes and one back toe, or spur, like a rooster. Its snout was the only thing lean and long about it, and lining that long mouth were razor-sharp teeth, each the length of my hand. Its eyes, slanted like a cat, gleamed a purplish light.

The beast stopped before us. Its snout was mere inches from Calum's chest, and I felt hopeful as it didn't eat us immediately.

Small wisps of smoke rose from its nostrils, and it sniffed Calum slowly, eyes blinking. A low rumble rose from its chest, and I wasn't sure whether it was a growl or a sigh.

Calum answered my thoughts. "She won't hurt us. She's just thankful she's free, and she says we don't have to worry about those soldiers anymore."

I looked at the beast before us, and she watched me, her eyes penetrating my own. She didn't move as Calum reached forward, placing her hand on her snout.

"May we approach?" Reuben's voice rose from behind us.

Calum turned and smiled. "Of course."

They stumbled forward, Reuben's arm wrapped around Darius's waist as he was unsteady on his feet. Darius held one of his arms cradled in his other. It looked broken. His face was scrunched up in pain.

THE THINGS OF NATURE

"A tree landed on me," Darius explained, his voice faltering. "In the explosion."

The beast grunted, and Calum gave a soft smile. "She says she is sorry."

Reuben looked at her inquisitively. "Is she speaking to you?"

Calum shrugged. "Well, no, I understand her. Like, I know what she would want me to say."

"Incredible." Reuben brought Darius to stand beside us. "I've never seen a real dragon before, certainly not this close."

So, it was a dragon. I eyed her more carefully. I probably hadn't realized what she was because she hadn't breathed any fire yet. That had been the extent of my knowledge. Of course, I hadn't thought there was such a thing as dragons before, so I had no reason to study them or any other kind of magical creature. There were probably more creatures out there than I even realized.

Calum continued to speak for the dragon, her hand still on her snout. "She also wants to apologize for assisting the General and his soldiers. All she wanted was to be free, and she knew the moment the General raised the sword to kill, she would be set free."

Reuben nodded. "So, you were the one helping them move so quickly. It all makes sense now."

"Her magic was limited while she was trapped, but she did what she could."

Calum smiled, and as if she were speaking to the dragon in her mind, her brow furrowed as she cocked her head to the side. "She says that she is willing to take me far from here. Just me."

I spoke up, confused. "Where?"

"She says somewhere safe, where no one will ever hunt me again."

I struggled with that for a moment. "Just you?"

"Yes."

Silence reigned.

I was afraid she really would take the dragon's offer. But after all we had been through, I couldn't let go. I had just killed a man, and I had done it for her, for both of us. The whole adventure I had done for her, to keep her safe.

"Calum." I stepped forward, taking a deep breath. "Before you make a decision, I would like for you to hear me out for a moment."

Her eyes turned to me in curiosity. "Alright."

I took in a deep breath and let it out. I could do it, I told myself. I had to tell her how I felt and tell her how much she meant to me. I could be strong again like when I had killed the General. I could convince her and show her I *was* someone.

"Please, don't leave. The General is gone. The threat is eliminated." I took her hand, the one not on the dragon's snout. I squeezed it between my own and looked deep into her eyes.

"Do you remember Anthony? Do you remember how he left this earth to be with the one he loved?"

Calum nodded.

"You said that he hadn't left, he had gone home to her, because she *was* his home. I guess what I am trying to say, Calum, is that you're my home, too. When our house burned down, I only felt relief because I still had you. Those times we were about to die, I thought that as long as I died with you, then I wouldn't have to live alone, without you. What I'm saying is, that I will follow you to the end of the earth. I'll follow you wherever you go. Just please don't leave, please."

Her eyes were wide as she saw me—truly saw me.

"Adric," she spoke my name softly. "You really feel this way?"

"I do," I answered with pure conviction.

Her eyes bore into me. She was finally seeing me, but it was like I was something she had never expected. She was finally understanding me for the first time, and I surprised her. I was different from what she had always seen me as.

Finally, she took in a deep breath and let it out. "If I stay . . . I want things to be different."

"Anything," I answered easily.

"I don't want to hide anymore; not like we were in the village. I want to use my magic, too."

I nodded vigorously. "Of course."

All of that would be easy to do. We were leaving this place and we were never coming back.

"One last thing," she added.

"What is it?"

"No more hunting."

I grinned, almost laughing at how easy it was. "It's a deal."

She smiled, then turned back to the dragon. "I'm sorry, but I just can't."

The dragon blinked in recognition.

Calum spoke. "She says that she is willing to carry us across the mountains if that is still the direction we wish to travel."

I let out a breath of relief. It was true. I would be lost without her. She was my home, and I decided at that moment that I would continue to show her that I meant it. I had meant every word. I would not be the same person who cowered behind my doubts.

Reuben's grip tightened on Darius. "If she is willing, then we would be eternally grateful. We need to get Darius to a healer."

He didn't look good. His face was draining of color, and it looked like he might pass out from the pain.

Calum nodded. "She says to hurry. If he passes out on her back, she won't be able to both catch him and keep us on her back at the same time."

"Don't pass out," Reuben commanded.

"I'll try my best," Darius huffed.

Calum went first, clambering onto the dragon's back. She situated herself between two spikes, and she looked snug. As long as none of us fell sideways, we should be able to stay on.

The light of morning was now graying the sky, and after helping Darius up, I climbed on. I could feel the dragon breathing under me, and she was warm enough that I supposed there had to be a fire in her belly. I was able to squeeze the spike in front of me with both of my hands, but they were just long enough that I wouldn't be able to hold Calum in front of me. I'd only be able to reach out and grab her if she slipped, but that wouldn't happen, not now that we were finally leaving that place.

We were finally free of the General.

The sky continued to lighten, and it chased away the shadows surrounding us.

The forest around us was indeed destroyed by what had occurred. Splintered trunks and branches with new spring leaves created a carpet of destruction for about a quarter of a mile in every direction. The soldiers lay mostly hidden, buried beneath the leaves and sticks. Perhaps the dragon had consumed the survivors. They indeed would not bother us again.

"She says to hold on," Calum called from in front of me, and the dragon unfurled her wings.

They were thick, also covered in black scales, and I found myself thinking back to the wanderers' camp. I thought back to the story the storyteller had told us, and I realized that perhaps the story had some truth to it after all. By no means did I think Calum or I were heroes in the story of the dragon, but we had defeated the evil king and we were riding away, free and victorious.

In our story, I realized that there was bad magic and good magic, and there were good men and evil men. But even then, people like the witch and Lucian were not all entirely good or evil. They were a mix of the two. It was complicated. Not everything was black and white as I had previously assumed.

I also learned that it was important to have friends. The more, the better. We had barely made it out of the village in the beginning when we had been alone. They had all saved us on our journey, and without them, I couldn't imagine where we would still be.

The dragon gave several flaps of her wings, and the whoosh of air stirred the forest. Then, she leaped into the air in one big leap, and I almost felt my spine snap with the force, but then we were in the sky. Her wings continued to flap in mighty gusts, and I gripped the spike in front of me as we fell down, then up, repeatedly. The wind beat at my face as the ground fell away beneath us.

I had to squint my eyes against the wind, but I could now see the sun. It was rising over the mountains, its rays stroking the village and lands below.

Everything looked so small. All of our troubles were fading below as we now sped toward the jagged peaks. The only thing that worried me was Cassius. It wasn't likely, but I hoped he had made it. It made me sad to think we were leaving him and the others behind, but we were going somewhere unknown. We'd be able to make a *real* fresh start. We'd be able to discover just how big the world really was.

I felt hope inside of me as I watched Calum's back, her curls flicking in the wind. When we reached our destination, I hoped we could find a new home and build a new life for ourselves. I hoped we could make more friends and not have to hide anymore. Since she finally understood how I felt toward her, perhaps she would also come to reciprocate those feelings. She had truly come into herself with her magic and her courage. When her eyes glowed green, it was like her very soul shining through. She was, indeed, a thing of nature.

Want to read a novella for free?
Find out about Reuben and the beginning of his journey.
Simply join my newsletter here to join my mailing list and claim your free copy of this novella!
www.authormollyjane.com

Acknowledgments

I wish to begin by thanking my twin sister. Without you, this book would not be nearly as good as it is. The harshest critiques make for the best improvements, and even with your ridiculously busy schedule, you still found time for me. So, thank you for that.

I also wish to thank my other two beta readers, being my mother and my coworker. Thank you for your encouragements and making me feel like my book was not utter trash. Imposter syndrome is real, but you helped me realize I *do* belong and I *am* good at this!

Thank you also to my husband, who helped me to see that there is no time like the present to make my dreams come true.

The deepest, most important thanks I have, are for my grandmother. Where would I be without your stories? Where would I be if you had not sparked my imagination?

You are the reason I began making up my own stories when I was still tiny. You are also the one who introduced me to the idea of being a librarian. I cannot imagine where I would be if you hadn't. There is no job more perfect in the world than being a librarian. So, thank you for shaping and making my entire life a dream come true.

Finally, thank you to my cats. You keep me sane, and when I am dying internally, I can just inhale your fluffy perfection and immediately feel better.

Thank you for reading my book! If you liked it,
then please support me and leave a review on amazon!
It's greatly appreciated!

Made in the USA
Middletown, DE
13 October 2024